# MERRY MURDER

To Addison
Fiona's on the case.

Best
CS McDonald

# MERRY MURDER

## A Fiona Quinn Mystery

C.S. McDonald

ISBN-13: 9780991368082
ISBN-10: 0991368088

For my grandmother, Evelyn Stacy-Schibner-Burrell, no she never lived in our attic, but she will forever live in my heart.

Grandma always made you feel she had been waiting to see just you all day and now the day was complete.
~Marcy DeMaree

# Acknowledgements

Beta reader: Linda Taylor
Editorial Reviewer: Lauren Carr
Editor: Sherri Good, Silver Lining Editing Services
Cover design: Dawne Dominique, Dusk til Dawn Designs

I would like to thank all of these wonderful people listed above for their hard work to make this book possible.

## One

The front door opened quickly. Much too quickly for Fiona Quinn. The surplus of Christmas packages she was attempting to carry into the house in one trip spilled over the floor of the foyer. Her time-saving, effort-saving management plan hadn't been successful at all. Fiona tripped, falling against the door jamb, dropping her load. Several of the errant packages landed on the top of her dog Harriet's kennel. Harriet was not pleased by the sudden crash of objects, bouncing off the caging above her head. The tiny eight pound white Maltese growled and barked her reprimand, while cowering in the farthest corner of her confines.

Fiona dispelled a beleaguered sigh at her epic failure, as she pushed up from her knees to a standing position. She shrugged out of her cardigan sweater, pitching it on the hook just inside the door.

"Poor Baby. Sorry, Harriet." She set straight to gathering the packages and piling them on the stairs just beyond the kennel, while a clearly disgruntled Harriet paced back and forth, whining. "Okay, okay, gimme a minute. I'll let you outside after I pick these up so you won't have to climb over them. It would be better if this was it, but I've got way more shopping left, and very little time to do it."

After the last gift had been placed on the pile, Fiona kept her promise. She opened the kennel gate, and Harriet scampered out the front door, which her mistress had left standing wide open. Fiona stretched her back, then meandered to the door to watch the dog sniff the unusually green grass in the front yard. It was one week before Christmas and not a single snowflake had fallen in the Pittsburgh area. The temperatures had been above normal throughout the fall. Thanksgiving had been down right balmy. The weather was acting more like Florida than Pennsylvania, and the weatherman wasn't giving any hope of a white Christmas.

While Harriet was busy in the yard doing her thing, Fiona turned to gaze at the large Christmas tree in the living room. She loved Christmas. She loved the smell of fresh pine wafting throughout the downstairs of her childhood home. She'd purchased the big drafty house at 529 Oxford Street from her parents when they retired and moved to an 'over fifty-five' community in Daytona Beach, Florida. They had moved to escape the harsh winters of the north. Oh, how they relished calling her on the phone to boast about the lovely seventy-degree weather they were enjoying during the month of January, while Pittsburgh would usually be bracing for yet another six inches of snow. Fiona didn't mind terribly much. She liked the snowy winters that were commonplace in Pennsylvania, especially at Christmastime.

Shoulders slumping, she sighed. It was looking like her parents wouldn't be making any of those boastful phone calls this year. Too bad. Her parents were coming home for the holiday, and she so wanted it to be nothing less than perfect—and yes, her idea of Christmas perfection included a generous blanket of snow.

She rearranged several ornaments on the tree so they hung in better symmetry to the other bulbs on the nearby branches. She was doing everything possible to make the house perfect, the cookies perfect, the decorations and the gifts perfect, as her mother always had. It was her turn now. She longed for Christmas to be like it was when she and her brother and her parents all lived together, except there wasn't a thing she could do about the weather. Wishing there was, she plugged in the twinkle lights draped on the tree to take in the jubilant colors and the big bold star on top. She loved that star. It had been in her family for years. It belonged to her Grandma Evelyn, who had passed away many years ago, yet her spirit still lived in the house.

While among the living, Evelyn had occupied the attic apartment on the third floor when Fiona was a young girl, except after her death, she didn't leave. She remained in the house. No, Evelyn wasn't in the practice of haunting. She simply looked after her family, and when they grew and left the house, she watched over Fiona, her unmarried granddaughter, who'd decided to stay.

Fiona never saw her grandmother floating down the hallway or lurking in a dark corner of a room. It wasn't quite like that. Evelyn let her presence be known by taking care of little things. There was always coffee brewing in the morning when Fiona woke, and the porch light was always on when Fiona returned home later than expected. Fiona felt that Evelyn was her guardian angel or guardian grandmother, as it were.

Oh, sometimes Evelyn could be a bit noisy. Sometimes it sounded as if she were moving furniture around in her apartment, which had been left just as it was when she was alive. Fiona's mother said she wanted Evelyn, her mother, to feel welcome. She didn't want her to feel they were waiting for her to leave so they could use the attic for some other purpose. That was the main reason Fiona bought the house from her parents—to make sure Evelyn could stay, and feel comfortable doing so, for as long as she wished. In a way Fiona was Evelyn's guardian angel too—she'd kept the house so that Evelyn's spirit would be protected

Pulling her from her muse, a flash of red caught her eye outside the window. She tenderly pushed a branch from the tree aside, and craned her neck to look out the big picture window that lent a nice view over Oxford Street. Great Uncle Wilbur was making his way up the walk, sporting his Santa Claus costume. Following him along the sidewalk, Harriet danced around the old fellow's feet. Wilbur paused halfway to turn and wave merrily at the wide eyed, slack jawed children who were peering out their windows amazed to see Santa strolling along Fiona Quinn's sidewalk. They waved back, feverishly. Lord love him, Wilbur never missed an opportunity to make children smile or to promote the noble cause of Santa.

Fiona had to giggle to herself. From now on the children in the neighborhood would see her in a different light—she knew Santa Claus personally! Maybe they'd think twice about soaping her windows on Halloween—one could only hope.

Wilbur was grandma Evelyn's older brother. He was ninety years young, had never been married, retired from the steel mill many years ago, and lived a block or so away on Guyland Street. He absolutely loved to play the role of Santa every year at Macy's Department Store in downtown Pittsburgh, until it closed. He was sad, but he had been such a popular Santa that the management at the Robinson Mall near the Pittsburgh airport scooped him up.

"It just isn't the same," Uncle Wilbur once told her. "But I guess I should be thankful that I'm still able to do what I love."

Wilbur only required a costume and a bit of puffing up—he wasn't particularly heavy. He was on the short side, five-foot-six, and on the thinner side as well. His pure white beard and white hair was his own. Throughout the non-holiday months, he kept the beard cut close to his face and his hair short. When November rolled around, all bets were off—the beard and his hair were left to their own devices. He was most accommodating to any child who wanted to take a quick tug of his beard to prove, without a doubt, that he was indeed the real Santa Claus. Like Fiona, Wilbur loved Christmas and all the hub-bub that surrounded the holiday. But what he loved most was making the children smile.

Harriet trotted along behind Wilbur through the front door. Scooping her up and patting her head, he peeked into the living room. "Are you in the habit of leaving the front door wide open? Any vagabond, like me, could walk right in," he said with a chuckle in his voice, enveloping Fiona in a warm hug.

Stepping back to take in his jolly appearance, Fiona said, "Wow. Your costume is very bright this year."

"It's brand-spanking new, and they just had it cleaned. The management from the character company decided that the suites were looking dull, so they gathered them all up the other day and sent them to the cleaner. Seven days before Christmas. I don't get it. They should've had it done before Thanksgiving. I thought they looked just fine." He shook his head. "Can't figure out management nowadays. They don't seem to do anything with commonsense in mind."

"Tell me about it. You should work for a school district," Fiona put in.

"No, thank you. Anyways, I wanted to pop in to find out when you're expecting your parents."

"I'm picking them up at the airport in about an hour."

Smiling, Wilbur stood back to admire her tree. "That's a great tree, Fiona. Looks beautiful from the street too. I can't believe that old star still lights."

"It sure does. Grandma Evelyn told me once that she'd bought it at the G.C. Murphy Store downtown."

"They don't make 'em like that anymore—stars or stores. I can guarantee that. Ev would be so pleased to know that you still use her Christmas star. I'm pretty pleased myself."

Fiona smiled. "Oh, I know she would. I guess from the way you're dressed, you're working tonight."

"Yep, not much time left. Gotta get those last Christmas requests recorded. I also dropped by to tell you that I'll stop in tomorrow to see your folks, if that's okay."

"Absolutely, Uncle Wilbur. Why don't you come for lunch? About twelve-thirty?"

"I'm working the late Santa shift at the mall tomorrow. Is it okay if I show up in my suit?"

Fiona laughed. "Are you kidding? We wouldn't have it any other way. Do me a favor, would you?"

"Anything for my favorite great niece."

"Bring my brother a chunk of coal. I have no doubt he's been naughty."

Chuckling, he gave her a quick peck on the cheek. "I've got a nice big piece with his name on it! I'll look forward to tomorrow. See you then." He set Harriet's feet to the floor, plopped his Santa cap on his head, winked at his great niece, and hurried out the door, making a big show of closing it behind him.

The star on the tree blinked three times.

—w—

Fiona circled the Pittsburgh International Airport several times searching for her parents. She pulled over in the pickup area and paused for a short time then made the circle again when she saw a police cruiser coming through. Like so many airports, vehicles were not permitted to linger for long periods of time for security reasons. She was growing concerned because her parents should have been through luggage claim and waiting for her in the pickup area, but they had yet to appear. Fiona's frustration was quickly transforming into worry. Had they missed their flight? Pulling to the side of the road, she checked her text messages. Nothing since earlier in the morning after her mother's text announcing that they were on their way to the airport.

Finally after the seventh pass, her parents were standing in the pickup station surrounded by their luggage. Fiona was relieved, but then, just as quickly, her brows furrowed. She slowed her Mini Cooper to make sure she was seeing what she thought she was seeing—along with their luggage, her mother and father also had five travel kennels. What? Those couldn't be her parent's kennels. Surely they belonged to someone else. Only there was no one else standing in the area, other than a security guard smoking a cigarette.

Yep, the closer she got, it was looking more and more like the kennels belonged to her parents. How was she going to fit the luggage, the kennels, and her parents in her tiny car? Worse, how was she going to accommodate five more dogs or whatever was inside the travel kennels? Yikes! Christmas was becoming a little more complicated than she had planned—way more complicated.

Fiona's father waved his hands over his head, with a bright smile stretched across his face, while her mother rolled up on tippy-toes, waving at her to make sure she saw them. Oh, she saw them all right. Mom, Dad, two carry-on cases, two large suitcases, and five kennels filled with dogs. Suddenly she felt a tinge of panic coil through her stomach. Wait a minute. She couldn't see what was inside the kennels—they were enclosed.

What if there weren't dogs in the kennels?

What if they'd decided to get some kind of exotic pets, like... *Ferrets?*

Oh God, what if they had five kennels filled with ferrets?

She rolled her eyes in self-reprimand. She hadn't even pulled up to the curb and she was thinking the worst. *Calm down already. It's Christmas. No matter what's in those kennels, you're gonna have to make the best of it.* She slowed the Mini Cooper to a stop in front of her visitors, while feigning an enthusiastic smile and an even more enthusiastic wave.

Jumping from the car, she called out, "Hi, Mom, Dad."

Her parents took her into a tight hug. Her father kissed her on the top of her head, while Mom kissed her cheeks. She was happy to see them looking so healthy—and tanned.

Her father, Garrett Quinn, was tall and thin. His brown hair had only a hint of grey at his temples. Her mother, Nancy, was shorter and also rail thin. Her red hair had no grey at all—thanks to Miss Clairol. She looked wonderful with only a few laugh lines on her face. Fiona had to chuckle to herself. It was sixty degrees out, yet they were bundled up in coats and scarves as if it were thirty below.

"How's my favorite kindergarten teacher? Those kids treating you good?" Her father asked, giving her one last squeeze before releasing.

"I'm good. The kids are a little over the top right now with Christmas right around the corner. Let's just say I'm ready for the holiday break."

"When does it start?" he asked around a snort.

"Wednesday—three more days of class, but who's counting?"

"Fiona," her mother began. "You're so painfully thin. Aren't you eating properly?"

"I—"

"Nancy, she looks wonderful. Don't fuss. It's Christmas," he scolded.

"I'm not fussing. I just want her to eat properly. I don't want her to be one of those anorexics."

"I'm not—"

7

"I don't think she looks at all anorexic. She's just thin. You were unbelievably thin when you were in your twenties." He turned to his daughter. "You're still in your twenties, aren't you?"

"Yes, Dad. I'm—"

"So what are you saying, Garrett? I'm not thin anymore? I walk five miles a day with the community walking club. I take water aerobics twice a week, and a yoga class on Thursdays. I eat salads like I'm a rabbit, grilled chicken salad; chop salad; steak salad, and grilled salmon salad. I'm so sick of lettuce I could just scream. What more would you have me do?"

"I think you look—"

"I didn't say that you were fat, Nancy. I just said that you were *painfully* thin, like Fiona, when you were young, like Fiona."

"So!" Fiona interrupted loudly, while pointing at the kennels. "What have we got here? You didn't tell me that you were bringing pets along."

"We wanted to surprise you with our new little family," her mother said, bending down to peek into one of the kennels. Fiona looked in too, finding sheer relief when a chorus of barking welcomed them. Wagging their tiny tails, five little Yorkies looked back at them.

"That's what took us so long to get through baggage claim," Dad explained. "I hope you don't mind us bringing them along."

"No, no, it'll make the holidays a bit more…interesting." Fiona added under her breath, "Or chaotic."

"Intros!" Mom announced. Pointing to each kennel, as she added, "This is John, and George, and Paul, that's Ringo, of course. Can't you tell? He's got the biggest snout of them all."

"Of course," Fiona muttered.

"You know how your mother always *loved* the Beatles," Dad said with way too much tolerance in his tone.

"No, no I didn't realize—"

Coming to the last kennel, Mom said, "And last but never least, Keith."

"As in Keith Richards?" Fiona asked as if it were as obvious as the sun rising in the morning.

Befuddled, Mom tilted her head to one side. "No, what would make you say that?"

Fiona's eyes widened. "Um…As in the Rolling Stones? *Keith Richards* of the *Rolling Stones*?"

Mom waved a dismissive hand. "Oh, goodness no. Keith Schlemmer was my fiancé before your father. I thought the puppy looked like him, so the name just stuck."

Dad leaned in close to Fiona. "The name sticks in my craw, and she knows it."

"Well, I'm sure we'll make it all work…*Somehow*. But how are we getting everything home? My car won't hold the luggage, the kennels, and three adults."

"I've called a van to pick me and kennels up," Dad said. "You take the suitcases and your mom. I'll catch up. It should be here any minute."

A police cruiser drove past slowly. The officer was giving them the eye. Fiona quickly suggested, "We'd better get moving. I'm only allowed to park here for a few minutes or they'll ticket me."

Dad loaded the Mini Cooper with the luggage and carry-on cases. Soon Fiona and her mother were on their way home to begin the hap-happiest season of all—hopefully.

## Two

The door opened quickly. Much too quickly for Garrett Quinn. His attempt to carry three kennels in at one time failed. He twisted and turned to regain control of the tumbling cases so the dogs would not be harmed. He caught them with the tips of his fingers. He caught them with his chin and shoulders. His legs and his knees. He managed to break their fall, but not his own.

"Dad! Are you okay?" Fiona cried, as she hurried toward the sound of the crash in the foyer.

Holding on to the chunky square newel at the bottom of the staircase, while rubbing his back, he slowly climbed up from the floor. "I'm gonna be a little stiff for a while, but I think I'm good. Are the dogs okay?" he asked over the rouse of panicked barking coming from inside the kennels. Tail wagging zealously, Harriet scampered from the living room to sniff, growl, and yip at the holiday guests, while Fiona set to checking the dogs' well-being.

"Where would you like me to put these?" a man's voice asked from the doorway.

Fiona and her father looked up to see the van driver holding two kennels, while crinkling his nose in disdain. Fiona said, "Oh, just put them right there. Thank you for carrying them in."

The driver shrugged. "He paid me extra." With that he set the kennels down, adjusted his turban, and walked out the door.

"Merry Christmas," Fiona called after him as she closed the door. Flipping his hand in a feeble wave, the man kept going without looking back.

Gingerly, he bent down to open the kennels. One by one the little Yorkies bounded from their cages to sniff, growl and circle Harriet. Each one donned a colorful Christmas collar with a silver name tag dangling from the itty-bitty hitch. "Okay, this is George, and here comes Ringo. Your mom's right, he does have a big snout." Dad chuckled. He continued to open kennels. "John and Paul, and this one's Keith."

"They're adorable," Fiona said with a giggle in her voice.

"I doubt you'll be saying that in a week or so. You'll be ready for them and us to leave."

"Don't be silly. I'm so happy that you decided to come home for Christmas." Growling low and terse, Harriet sniffed Keith. He returned the favor. "That's Keith," Fiona told the Maltese. Cocking her head in a befuddled manner, Harriet looked up at her mistress. Fiona assured, "No, not that Keith."

The Yorkies all trotted off to explore their new environment. Harriet was right on their tails. There was some growling and a little nipping in the doggy way to get acquainted with one and other, or perhaps to determine a fresh pecking order. Fiona was confident, or at least hopeful, they'd settle down after a while.

"We'll keep them in their kennels at night. Where's your mother?" Dad asked.

"I dunno. I haven't seen her for about twenty minutes or so. Maybe she's upstairs unpacking. There's coffee in the kitchen if you'd like some. I'll go find her."

Her father seemed more than pleased to get coffee rather than look for his wife, Fiona noted, as she climbed the stairs. The bathroom was the first room at the top of the stairs—empty. The very next room used to be her parent's, and thusly, Fiona had groomed it for their visit—including fresh holiday flowers in a vase on the vanity and chocolates on the pillows. She wanted them to feel instantly welcome. The suitcases lay on the bed, unopened, however the bedroom was unoccupied. The next room had always been hers, and it still was. She thought perhaps her mother was in there, snooping around. Nope. The smallest room at the end of the hallway that used to be her brother's, but was now the computer room, was quiet too.

There was only one place left to look—the attic apartment. Grandma Evelyn's rooms.

The door to the attic was closed. If one was unfamiliar with the house, they would dismiss it as a closet. The stairs that led to the apartment was directly over the stairs that led to the second floor. Fiona opened the door to come face to face with the stair-lift still attached to the wall and on its track. Her parents had the one on the main staircase removed after grandma's death. Evelyn used the lifts for the last four or five years of her life. Her arthritic legs stopped her from climbing on her own accord, but her stubborn demeanor insisted that she could still live in the apartment on the third floor. There was no way she was going to move to a lower floor and disrupt the family's life style. God love her.

Fiona called up the stairwell, "Mom, are you up there?"

"Yes!"

Fiona jogged up the stairs to find her mother stripping the white sheets that covered Evelyn's furniture, tossing them into a laundry basket. "What are you doing?"

"It's obvious that you don't come up here very often. These sheets have an inch of dust over them. The place needs a good cleaning and vacuuming," Mom said with a hint of reprimand in her voice.

Fiona glanced around the large area. Evelyn's dresser stood between the two windows that looked out over Oxford Street. Her queen-size poster bed was against the far wall. An antique desk that she used to refer to as her "bill paying desk" was stationed in a small nook behind and to the left of the bed where a long window looked out onto the neighbor's roof. Fiona noticed that her ninth-grade school portrait and her brother's seventh-grade photo still sat on the desk in simple gold frames. The sunshine filtering through the window lent evidence of the years of dust gathered on the glass in the frames. An old white princess phone that had been disconnected after her death also remained.

About ten feet from the foot of the bed was her living room. Well, it wasn't exactly a living room, it was the space where her couch, winged back chair, and TV stand were positioned. The old analog

TV was still there, with a large knob to the right of the screen to change the channels, and four smaller knobs below for volume, color adjustments and so on. No remote, but there was a pair of rabbit ears sitting on top of the set. Fiona had to wonder if it would turn on after so many years.

Mom yanked a sheet off a green couch. Fiona remembered many a Sunday afternoon sitting on the couch next to Grandma Evelyn watching a movie. Grandma would have cookies and pop for her. They had some great conversations. She remembered watching *Gone with the Wind* for the first time on that very TV. She was mesmerized by the film and it was still one of her favorites.

"You don't mind, do you?" her mother asked, breaking through her memories.

"Mind what?"

"If we red-up the apartment? Mom wouldn't like all this dust and cobwebs. How often do you come up here?"

"I never come up and I never *clean it up* either. I don't think I've been up here since your last visit almost two years ago."

"Are you afraid to come up?"

"No. There's really no reason. I don't store anything in here."

Mom sat down on the couch. "She's still here, you know. I can feel her presence."

"She makes her presence known to me all the time. She's my guardian angel, but I consider this her private area, and I don't invade it."

"Well, I'll take these down the basement and throw them in the wash," Mom said. She picked up the basket, and they made their way downstairs. "When is your brother coming?"

"Chad will be here for lunch tomorrow. Oh, and I invited Uncle Wilbur too."

"How nice. Sounds like we'll have a full house. Chad, Uncle Wilbur, and the young man you've been seeing—that detective, what's his name again?"

"Nathan, Nathan Landry."

"Has a nice ring to it, Nathan Landry—*Fiona Landry*. I like it."

"*Seriously?*"

—⁓—

*SportsCenter* was all abuzz about the Steelers game coming up on Sunday evening. Not that Garrett could actually hear what the commentators were saying—the dogs were still chasing each other through the house, while yapping and yipping, accompanied by a random yelp every five minutes or so. It was becoming mind-numbing. The low hum overhead reverberating from the vacuum cleaner on the third floor was compounding the distractions. Letting out a worn-out sigh, he turned the TV off, tossed the remote aside, and decided to read the newspaper. He remembered seeing one lying on the porch steps while carrying in the kennels earlier in the day. He also recalled a plate of Christmas cookies carefully guarded by a snug canopy of plastic wrap, sitting on the counter between Fiona's crockpot and the coffee maker. The sweet snacks were calling his name, and he was definitely in the mood for a tasty fix—especially with Nancy upstairs, unaware of his indulgence.

The alluring smell of something wonderfully meaty cooking in the crockpot wafted through the downstairs. Garrett pushed up from the couch and went into the kitchen where George and Ringo were devouring Harriet's food. He lifted the lid of the crockpot to take a whiff of the roast Fiona was slow-cooking for dinner. Mmmm.

Eyeing the cookies, he refilled his coffee cup. The vacuum had stopped. He stilled, listening for a moment, and then furtively glanced over his shoulder. The vacuum started again. He snatched several cookies from the plate, then replaced the plastic wrap. Merrily whistling Jingle Bells, he made his way down the short hall, through the foyer, and out the door with Keith on his heels.

Ah, there it was, his old friend, The Pittsburgh Post-Gazette. Anxious to catch up on all the latest happenings in the Burgh, he gathered the paper from the steps, hurried into the house, closing the door behind him—leaving Keith outside.

—⁓—

Eyes narrowed, hands on hips, while searching around the kitchen where the other four Yorkies and Harriet were busy gathering around the food dishes, Mom asked, "Where's Keith?"

Fiona was busy checking on the roast in the crockpot.

Dad was sitting at the table reading the paper with his third cup of coffee sitting in front of him.

More aggressively, Mom repeated, "*Where's* Keith?"

Dad looked up from the sports section. "I'm sure he's around. He's been fussing with the other dogs all afternoon."

Fiona looked up from the crockpot to see her mother searching under the table, the chairs, and walking down the hall in pursuit of the little dog, while mumbling under her breath.

"He's got to be here, Mom. We haven't left the house since you got here. Although I think the dogs could probably use a visit to the yard."

Obvious frustration filling her tone, expression, and stance, Mom stated, "Well, he's not here. He's not anywhere. Has anyone gone outside? He could've slipped through without being noticed." Her right eyebrow raised at the sight of Dad and his newspaper. "Where did you get *that?*"

"On the porch steps, but he didn't come out with me," Dad said.

The alarm in Mom's voice was rising at a steady rate. "How can you be sure? I mean, he's missing for God's sake. I hope there wasn't a cat outside. He hates cats. He'll chase them until his little paws bleed."

"I think I would've noticed if the dog followed me outside—especially if he took off after a cat. I'm not blind, Nancy."

"I'm not so sure, Garrett, but you do lean toward the irresponsible side at times. You lost Ringo in the park just last week." She glanced out the window. "And it's getting dark outside!"

"That was different. It's hard to keep an eye on five dogs in a public place. If you hadn't been gossiping with Claire Boyer, I wouldn't have had to watch all five of them. Everywhere we go you get involved in a long drawn-out conversation with someone or other, leaving me to care for the chil—*dogs* on my own. Besides, there were no cats involved."

"Of course not. We were in a *dog park*. Oh, never mind that. We've got to go find him. He's probably terrified. What if he's been hit by a car! You know how people fly down Oxford Street. The cat could've ran out in front of the car to get away, and Keith followed, only he didn't make it. Fiona, call your boyfriend the policeman!"

"He's a homicide detective, Mom, not the dog catcher."

"We need to form a search party," Mom insisted.

"That seems a little over the top. I think we need to stay calm," Fiona said, trying to quell her mother's rising anxiety. "Don't worry, we'll find Keith—"

Just then the doorbell rang. *Saved by the bell*, Fiona thought as she hurried to the door, as did the remaining Yorkies and Harriet, while trying to out-bark each other. She didn't recognize the man on the other side, but he was holding a shivering little Yorkie in his arms.

"Sorry to bother you, miss, but I've been going door to door with this little dog. Do you know who he belongs to?" the man asked.

Fiona let out a relieved breath, but before she could get out a word, Mom rushed forward with arms open wide. "Keith! You found my Keith!" She took the dog from the man's arms to cuddle him close to her chest. Keith licked her cheeks. "Thank you so much for bringing him back."

"*Nancy?*" the man inquired.

Fiona's mom's eyes met the stranger's. Recognition suddenly flooding her gaze. "Keith? Oh my goodness, could it be *Keith Schlemmer?*"

Even over five dogs yapping, Fiona heard her father let out a lurid sigh. He mumbled under his breath, "*Great. Just great.*"

"Nancy Burrell, you look amazing! I didn't know that you still lived in this house. How could I have missed that? I moved into the house three doors down about six months ago."

Fiona was almost embarrassed by the blush on her mother's cheeks—it was positively brilliant. Her father's cheeks were turning red as well, but in a different way. Not a good way.

"Come in, come in and sit down," Mom said, setting Keith, the dog, down and looping her arm through Keith Schlemmer's arm. "I'd love to catch up. What are you doing nowadays?"

"I own a dry-cleaners in Robinson Township with my brothers, Bobby and—"

"Are you married, children?"

"No, I'm afraid I never married." He chuckled. "You broke my heart, Miss Burrell."

"Mrs. *Quinn*," Dad spoke up.

"Oh, Keith, you remember my husband, Garrett," Mom said.

The two men locked eyes. Slowly and tentatively they shook hands. Fiona feared the simple handshake might turn into an arm wrestling match.

Keith quickly said, "Well! I'm glad you got your dog back, Nancy. Is his name really Keith?"

Mom nodded in a flirty manner. Fiona could feel the blush rising on her own cheeks.

Keith, the man, snorted. "How funny. Well, I've got to get going. I'm late for my shift at the dry-cleaners. I own a rather large, *very* successful dry-cleaning business in Robinson—"

"Yeah," Dad groaned. "You've mentioned that already."

Keith's face reddened. He wrung his hands. "Well, it was so nice to see you again. Now that I know you live just three doors up, perhaps I'll bump into you more often."

"That would be *great*," Dad said, wryly.

Keith hurried to the door with Mom on his heels. "Hope to see you soon. Thanks again for bringing the dog back. Oh! And have a merry Christmas!" she called after him, closing the door.

"Mom, why didn't you tell him that you don't live here anymore?"

"What? I didn't tell him that I live here. Why would he think that I'm living here?" Mom said in a dismissive manner, as she made her way back to the kitchen with a pack of pint-size dogs trotting after her.

"Oh, I dunno, maybe because you lived here for most of your life," Fiona said under her breath.

Watching her mother's retreat, Fiona felt a little taken aback. Seriously? Was the woman so mesmerized by her former lover—what? Yuck! She shook that vision right out of her head. Was her mom so struck by Keith Schlemmer's impromptu visit that she barely heard a word that he'd said? Yikes.

She turned to gauge her father's reaction. He plunked down on the couch, picked up the remote and started flipping through the channels. He was clearly irritated by the entire Keith kerfuffle. She twisted several strands of strawberry blond hair between her fingers. It would appear that her parent's holiday visit may become more eventful than she originally thought. Hm, it was beginning to look a lot like Christmas.

Fiona's parents barely spoke a word to each other the rest of that evening. There seemed to be a lot of frustrated sighs exchanged and even more unpleasant askance glances, but on the upside, the roast was delicious. Even still, she was thankful when the day ended. The Yorkies were tucked away in their kennels and Harriet was snoring under the blankets at her feet. It had definitely been an exhausting day for everyone, human and canine. Tomorrow would most likely be as tiring and stressful—her parents would meet Detective Nathan Landry, her boyfriend, for the first time. Double yikes!

## Three

Breakfast with her parents had been as icy as December should be. The breakfast table was null and void of conversation. Luckily, the air instantly cleared upon the arrival of her younger brother, Chad. By the time Uncle Wilbur showed up her parents were back to laughing and joking. The dog's vanishing act, and Keith Schlemmer's visit appeared to be forgotten. Joy to the World!

The delicious smells of turkey roasting in the oven and fresh baked apple pie drifted through the house, reminding Fiona of the many Thanksgivings and Christmas' past. Even though Christmas Eve was still four days away, she wanted to have a special luncheon for the family—and Nathan. She and her mother were just putting the finishing touches on the dining room table when there was a knock at the door. Fiona stilled.

Mom's gaze snapped to meet her daughter's. A wide smile stretching across her face, she said, "There's only one guest who hasn't arrived yet—your policeman boyfriend."

"He's a homicide detective, and I'd appreciate it if everyone would at least *try* to act normal," Fiona said, setting down the napkins to make her way to the door only to find her father, and Uncle Wilbur, who was sporting his Santa pants and boots and a bright red T-shirt. Yeah, Nathan wouldn't think that was too terribly strange. Oh well, Uncle Wilbur's attire would most likely be just one of a long string of strange things Nathan would witness during lunch.

Chad and all the dogs joined the throng of family members crowded in the foyer. The men had mischievous grins plastered on their faces, which were a bit disturbing—almost as disturbing as Uncle Wilbur's Santa attire, but at least they weren't barking and dancing in place, like you-know-who.

"Seriously? Can't you guys wait in the living room so he doesn't feel like he's facing a firing squad?"

"Aw, c'mon, Sis, this is the first boyfriend you've ever introduced to the family," Chad goaded.

Fiona pointed a cautionary finger at the group. "There's probably a good reason for that, so don't make me sorry. *Behave.*"

"I dunno, guys. She seems really nervous. I wonder what's wrong with him," Chad said, pure orneriness filling his tone.

"*Chaaad—*"

"*Fi-on-aaa—*"

"Don't make me hurt you," Fiona warned.

"Just open the door, Fiona," Mom insisted. "The poor man's probably freezing to death."

"It's fifty-eight degrees."

"Open the door!" the group sang out in unison.

After fluffing her hair with her fingers, and on a braced breath, Fiona opened the door. Detective Nathan Landry was greeted by an overture of barking and a small crowd of strangers wearing expectant grins—except for Fiona, she looked rather stressed.

He smiled. "Hello, Ms. Quinn. I'm looking forward to that turkey you've been telling me about all week." He presented one of the glittery potted poinsettias he was holding. "I brought this for you, and I brought one for your mom, too."

"Well, aren't we trying hard to make a good impression?" Fiona teased, depositing a quick kiss on his cheek.

"You only get one chance," he said. The dogs danced and yipped around his ankles. He scooped Harriet up on his way through the door. "Hey, Harriett, who are all your little friends?"

"Oh, you'll find out soon enough." Fiona followed him inside where he came face to face with the family.

Fiona giggled to herself when Nathan almost took a step back. She was proud of him when he bravely kept forward momentum through the door. Presenting the only woman in the cluster with the other poinsettia, he said, "I'm assuming you're Fiona's mom, Nancy. My mom always says it's important to bring something for the hostesses of a dinner. Merry Christmas, Mrs. Quinn."

Fiona thought that her mom looked almost as charmed by Nathan as she was with Keith Schlemmer. Her smile stretched all with up to her fairy green eyes.

She whispered to Fiona. "Have you met his mother?"

"No."

After shooting her daughter a surprised glance, Mom took Nathan into a big hug. "I'm so glad to finally meet you, Nathan. We've heard so much about you. Fiona doesn't tell us much about her love life. You must be a keeper."

"*Mom—*"

Nathan chuckled. "I certainly hope so, Mrs. Quinn."

"Please, call me Nancy."

Fiona quickly proceeded to introduce her family, and then it was time for the dogs. "That one, the one with the longest snout, is Ringo. And then there's Paul, and John and that one's George."

"Someone likes the Beatles," Nathan put in.

"I've always been a big fan," Mom said. She pointed to a Yorkie standing back from the pack. "That one over there is Keith."

"You mean like—"

"Don't—" Fiona attempted.

"Keith Richards…of…The…Rolling Stones?" Nathan asked.

Bowing her head while scrubbing her eyebrows with her fingers, Fiona let out a fraught sigh. She wished he would've kept that question to himself.

"Why does everyone keep asking me that?" Mom asked.

"Cuz it's ridiculously obvious," Chad said.

Stepping forward, Uncle Wilbur decided to change the subject. "I hear you're a police officer. Didja hear about that robb'ry last night in Crafton?"

"I'm a homicide detective, sir, I don't really know too much about robberies in the area, I'm afraid," Nathan explained.

"Someone broke into my friend, Paul Warner's house. He's one of the Santa's at the mall. Anyway, they made a real wreck of his place—only stole his Santa suit though. Strangest thing."

"That is strange," Nathan agreed.

"Ol' Paul called me this mornin' and asked if he could borrow my costume, but obviously, I needed it for my shift. Hope he found one for his shift. Those robbers better not come to my house or you'll know all about that *attempted* robb'ry for sure," Wilbur said, lifting his sagging chin to a haughty level. "Got me a .45 at home. It's all licensed and legal. Got a permit to carry, too. I could be a pistol-packin' Santa if I had a mind to. Hope it never comes to that."

Fiona cleared her throat, loudly. "On that Christmassy note, let's all gather around the table. Lunch is on."

On cue, everyone made their way through the living room toward the dining room. The two rooms were separated with a half-wall that Fiona had decked out in vibrant red silk poinsettias and soft white twinkle lights.

Fiona's dad followed Uncle Wilbur as he hobbled past the tree. The star blinked three times.

Dad said, "Uh-oh, looks like Evelyn's old star has a short in it. Maybe this is its last Christmas."

Fiona whirled around. "I hope not. I'd be heartbroken."

"I'll take a look at it when I get a chance. Hopefully it's nothing that can't be fixed with a little tweaking," Dad said.

"I hope it's something as simple as that," Mom began. "It blinked three times. Mom used to say that when something blinks three times or the wind knocks at the door or window three times, it means there's going to be a death."

Wilbur laughed, while raising his hand in a volunteer manner. "Well, I'm ninety. Maybe Evelyn's tellin' me it's time to come on home."

"Oh goodness, Uncle Wilbur, I don't think so. It was just an old wives tale she liked to scare us children with—and it was quite effective. Let's forget about it and have a nice lunch," Mom said, patting the old man on the back. She tossed Fiona a wary look.

Watching her family, and Nathan, passing the food and enjoying conversation did Fiona's heart good. It had been a long time since the family had sat at this very dining room table for a meal of any kind. The house seemed warmer somehow.

"Isn't this nice? To have the family gathered for a big meal?" Mom began. "It would be so much nicer if there were a few grandchildren at the table too."

Letting out a defeated sigh, Fiona rolled her eyes.

Dad took the opportunity to reminisce about how all the children in the neighborhood used to gather in their yard, the largest on the block, almost on a daily basis, for a hearty baseball game. Sometimes the games would go on and on until it was too dark to see the ball.

Mom reminded everyone of the sledding parties they used to host. The kids and adults would mount the sleds at the top of the yard, and if you could get the sled going fast enough and make the bend around the garage into the alley, you would fly all the way down onto Warriors Road.

"No one ever got hit by a car," Mom laughed. "I don't know why—we certainly deserved to. Of course, if we took our *grandchildren* sledding we would be more careful."

"*I don't believe it,*" Fiona grumbled under her breath.

"Oh, it's not that we didn't love them enough to be careful our own children, Nathan, we were just younger and less experienced with children than we are nowadays. Isn't that right, Garrett?"

"*Seriously,* Mom?" Fiona mumbled, burying her forehead in her hand.

Dad shrugged. "I suppose."

Chad shot Fiona an evil glance. She gulped back. What was he thinking? Her chest tightened. What was he going to share?

"Ya know, I think it's kinda funny that our Fiona has taken up with a cop," Chad said.

*Uh-oh. Here it comes!*

"Why is that?" Nathan inquired.

"She didn't tell you? *Fiona*, I can't believe you didn't tell Nathan about your life of crime—although she did manage to avoid a police investigation or arrest."

Frantically, Fiona searched her mind. What could he be talking about? She'd never been arrested. If there was one thing Chad loved it was to watch her sweat—to torture her. Even though he was almost three years her junior, he was very good at it. No—he was a pro.

"I don't know what you're talking about," Fiona said. She could feel the burn on her cheeks. She was positive she was as red as the Christmas tablecloth.

"Sure ya do. Remember Mr. and Mrs. Adams who lived above us?" He hitched his chin toward the house located at the top of the yard—the first house at the top of Oxford Street. "Don't you remember, they had a little white dog, like Harriet? You were in love with that dog. You were about seven, and I was prob'ly four. We used to go up to visit the dog and Mrs. Adams would give us candy—Hershey bars, I think."

Chad had everyone's undivided attention, including Nathan's. Fiona's spine stiffened against her chair. It was all coming back to her, and it wasn't a very nice memory. She'd forgotten all about the incident, most likely because it was so out of character for her, and terribly unpleasant, she'd buried it deep inside her subconscious.

There was nothing she could do now. Chad was going to spill the proverbial beans whether she wanted him to or not. She cleared her throat in a last ditch effort that he would take it as a signal that she'd prefer him to drop the subject.

"Yes, I remember the Adams', and I remember the little dog, but I don't remember there ever being a problem." Fiona looked up from her mashed potatoes to find her parents and Uncle Wilbur staring at her as if she'd just grown another head. Oh, good. They were going to confirm Chad's story when he finished telling it—that was *exactly* what she needed. "It's your story, Chad. Why don't you just tell it?" Fiona suggested.

"C'mon, how bad can it be?" Nathan asked. "It's Fiona, the kindergarten teacher, what could she have possibly done that was so bad?"

Chad laughed. "Wow! You've got him fooled!"

"Just tell the story, *Chad*," Fiona hissed through clenched teeth.

"Well, one day Fiona and I went up to visit old Mr. and Mrs. Adams, but they weren't home. Now, when we'd visit, we'd play with the little dog, and then Mrs. Adams would give us each a Hershey bar—full size. Anyway, we'd made the trip to their house several times and they hadn't been home. We couldn't figure out where they were, so we looked through the picture window. The glass jar where Mrs. Adams kept the candy bars was on the coffee table in the living room, we could see it from the window. Fiona kept knocking on the door, but no one came. She must'a wanted a candy bar really bad, because she picked up a rock from their landscaping and threw it through the window."

Chad paused long enough to check Nathan's reaction. Fiona glanced askance to see it too. Nathan had a svelte smile on his lips, while he continued to wolf down some stuffing drenched in gravy.

Looking around the table, Fiona noticed that everyone's eyes were on Nathan, waiting for his reaction.

Nathan said, "Wow. That is totally out of character for Fiona. What happened next?"

"I got in trouble. I got in big, big trouble," Fiona announced, tossing her hands in the air, feigning surrender.

"Oh, yeah," Chad laughed. "Turned out Mr. Adam's was in the hospital. He'd had a stroke. Mom dragged Fiona to the hospital to make her apologize to Mrs. Adams. Dad was furious. We had to pay for a new window, and let's just say we weren't welcome at Mrs. Adams's home ever again. Moral of the story: Fiona Quinn isn't as innocent as she appears. The kindergarten teacher has a past."

Once again, all eyes were on the police detective seated at the table. Nathan casually picked up his napkin and wiped the corners of his mouth. "Actually, I'm relieved to hear it. The story you just told leaves me off the hook, Chad. Thanks for sharing."

"Leaves you off the hook in what way?" Mom asked.

"Well, if there's one thing I've learned while being in the police department, it's that *everyone* has some sort of a past. Even an adorable kindergarten teacher, who I am very attached to, has made a few errors in judgement. I find that rather refreshing. My mom had her hands full when I was a kid, that's for sure. Fiona wouldn't want to know some of things I did when I was young and foolish. She prob'ly wouldn't want to date me, if she knew what I was capable of."

"I don't think that's true," Fiona told him, then she kissed his cheek. "But thank you for that."

Uncle Wilbur pushed from his seat to make his way around the table, while digging deep in his pocket.

Mom let out a charmed sigh. "I just think they're so cute together. I'll bet they'd have darling children."

"*Seriously*, Mom, stop—"

Just then Wilbur dropped something in Chad's lap.

Wearing a baleful expression, Chad held up a big chunk of coal. The room erupted in laughter.

After the dishes had been cleared, loaded in the dishwasher, and the dessert served, Fiona walked Nathan out to his car. Her heart swelled at the thought of how Nathan had stood up for her at lunch, but she was feeling sore at her brother for rehashing the embarrassing calamity from years ago.

"Aw, c'mon, Fiona. Don't be too mad at Chad for telling that story."

"Sometimes my little brother can be a real jerk," she growled.

Nathan snorted. "Remember, I have an older sister too. I've been guilty of acting like a jerk a time or two when she had a boyfriend visiting. That's what little brothers do. It's our job. It may even be our birthright."

"Really? Well, did you ever tell a story where your sister trespassed on private property and then did serious damage to said property?"

Nathan grimaced. "My sister would never do such a thing—that would be criminal." Fiona came to a dead stop. She blinked back. Her body stiffened. He chuckled at her aghast expression. "Look, you were a little girl. It happened a long time ago. You would never do anything like that now, as an adult—a kindergarten teacher."

She laughed. "That's pretty much a guarantee."

When Fiona returned inside the house she was surprised to find a stepstool pulled up to the Christmas tree. Across the room her father and her brother hovered over Grandma Evelyn's old star.

"Well, what' the verdict?" Fiona asked.

"We're going to try replacing all the twinkle lights inside the star. They're pretty old, and back in the day, if one light went out—they all went out. It's only blinking for now, but it may go out if one is going bad. Don't know if that's the problem, but it's the easiest solution, so we may as well try it first," Dad explained.

Fiona's dad and Chad gently tugged the old twinkle bulbs out of their sockets and even more gently pressed new ones into position. After forty-five minutes the star was put back together and ready to be returned to the top of the tree.

Chad climbed the stepstool and with quite a bit of fumbling around with the star, and his balance, he managed to get it back into position. Fiona, , and her parents watched as if he were performing major surgery. Finally the star was atop the tree.

Holding the plug to the star in his right hand, and the plug to the strands of lights in his left, Chad announced, "Well, here goes nothin'!"

He pushed the plugs together.

The star shone brightly.

They waited.

It stayed lit without blinking.

In unison, Fiona, and her parents let out a relieved sigh.

"See? It ain't over 'til the fat lady sings. Looks like we've got it fixed," Dad said.

"My mother was a tad on the chubby side, but I don't recall her ever singing," Mom whispered to Fiona, who shot her a baleful look in reply. Mom snorted, then favored her with a sly smirk.

"Sometimes I worry about you, Mom."

## Four

"There's no such thing as Santa Claus!" Lincoln Parrish shouted at two little girls whose eyes were tearing up at his harsh declaration.

"That's not true!" Lizzie Thomas shouted back. The freckles on her face were barely visible, as the angry red flush blended into them. "I saw him at the mall. I even pulled his beard. It was the *real* Santa!"

Hearing the fuss, Fiona made her way over to the children. "What's this all about?"

"Lincoln says that Santa's a fake, Miss Quinn!" Carly Barrows wailed, no longer able to hold her tears back. She pointed an accusing finger in the boy's direction, demanding, "Tell him that he's wrong!"

Carly's request placed Fiona in a bit of a debacle. Lincoln Parrish wasn't one of her favorite students. As a matter of fact, she really didn't like the little boy at all. He was a loud mouth, spoiled brat, who came from a wealthy family. Frankly, she was a little taken aback that his parents weren't buying into the whole Santa thing lock stock and barrel. Nonetheless, as a teacher, she wasn't in the position to tell the children to believe in anything, Santa, the Easter Bunny, Jesus or God. She wasn't permitted to support any religion or belief system.

Some of the teachers in the school would have Santa visit their classes during the Christmas parties, but that had to be cleared through the principal. Now she was being asked to endorse Santa Claus, and as much as she wanted declare him as real, she had to find a way around it.

While giving Carly a big hug, she told Lincoln, "Please take your seat. We'll be getting ready for bus calls soon."

In a huff, the boy marched to his seat and plopped down, crossing his arms over his chest, while scowling in Fiona's direction.

Ignoring him, she turned to the girls. "I'm glad to hear that you've visited with Santa, Lizzie. How about you, Carly, have you seen Santa yet?"

"No. Daddy said he'll take me tomorrow after school. If he has time." The child looked at her feet, as if she wasn't sure her dad would come through on his promise. Fiona's heart broke for her.

Lizzie tugged on Fiona's skirt, and asked, "Why doesn't Lincoln believe in Santa, Miss Quinn?"

"Well, the fact is Lincoln doesn't have to believe in Santa if he doesn't want to. But just the same, you can believe in anything or anyone that you want to."

Wiping her nose on the sleeve of her sweater, Carly inquired, "Do you believe in Santa, Miss Quinn?"

Thinking of her beloved great uncle, she confirmed, "I sure do. Maybe I can get him to visit our class before Christmas break."

The girls couldn't contain their joy. They jumped up and down, clapping their hands merrily. "I hope so, Miss Quinn!" Carly said. "That'll show ol' Lincoln Parrish a thing or two!"

So would a big box of coal, Fiona thought to herself. After meeting his parents several times she was most certain that wasn't going to happen—ever. She replied, "I said *maybe*. I have to clear it with Principal Britton. Now take your seats, girls. It's almost bus time."

"I hope he can come," Carly said, her face looking much brighter. "Then I'll get to see him for sure."

The closer Christmas drew, the more excitable her kindergarteners became, and the higher Fiona's stress levels rose. Teaching anything at all was becoming an exercise in, *forget it*. However, with December's weather being so mild, she was able to walk home from school. The short jaunt was a great stress reliever. Fiona was hoping the entire winter would be as mild so she could walk to and from home every day, as she did in the fall and spring months.

Once her class was safely loaded on their buses, she shrugged into her light jacket, shimmied into her backpack, tucked her dress shoes under her desk, and slipped on a pair of sneakers. She made her way through the schoolyard, down Guyland Street, past Uncle Wilbur's house—wait a minute. As his house came into view, so did the flashing lights from the police vehicles parked along Guyland, and in his driveway. The coroner's van was just pulling in as she stood directly across the street, shell shocked, from the house Grandma Evelyn once lived in, but sold to Uncle Wilbur when she moved in with Fiona's family.

While Fiona's brain was trying to process what was happening, her eyes fell upon Nathan's black SUV parked among the police vehicles in the driveway. She swallowed hard. Homicide Detective Nathan Landry was on the scene. That could only mean one thing—Uncle Wilbur or someone in his house had been murdered!

How could that be?

Why would anyone want to harm a ninety-year-old man—a *sweet* ninety-year-old man?

It was unthinkable. But clearly something very bad had happened at Uncle Wilbur's house. Fiona hurried across the street where a police officer stopped her before she stepped onto the driveway.

"I'm sorry, miss, we can't let you past," the officer explained, while blocking her way with his arm.

"This is my uncle's house. What's going on?" Fiona asked.

"Fiona!" A woman's voice called out. She and the officer turned to see Officer Tavia Andrews and Officer Wyatt Hays jogging toward them. They were both good friends of Nathan's and over the past ten months, they'd become her friends too. She loved Tavia. Her blonde hair curled around her face when she had her police hat on. Her eyes twinkled and her smile was always so bright, but at this moment, she was in police mode—nothing was twinkling or bright. She looked serious right down to the bone.

"It's okay, Mr. Stacy was this woman's uncle," Tavia told the officer.

"*Was?*" Fiona repeated. The simple three-letter word confirmed her worse fear, Uncle Wilbur was indeed dead. "What happened? Did he fall? Did he have a heart attack?"

Falling or having a fatal heart attack was bad, but not nearly as bad at being murdered—not in Fiona's mind.

"Nathan told us that Mr. Stacy was your uncle. So sorry for your loss, Fiona. Nathan's inside. He'll explain it all to you," Wyatt said, intentionally not making eye contact with her.

Tavia gave her a big hug. "C'mon, hun, we'll take you to him."

This was bad—very bad.

Fiona could see bad news in Tavia's eyes. Wyatt was still avoiding her gaze.

What was Nathan going to tell her?

She had a gut feeling that he hadn't fallen, and no, he didn't have a heart attack.

Her gut was telling her that dear Great Uncle Wilbur had been murdered.

Fiona shuddered.

What was she about to see?

They rounded the corner of the house, past dozens of officers milling about. They made their way across the patio where crime scene investigators were collecting who knows what, then they approached the kitchen door. Fiona's stomach twisted into tiny tight balls of knots. Her hands were shaking, except before they got to the door Nathan met them.

"Nathan!" Fiona called out.

Nathan grabbed her hands and squeezed. "I'm so sorry, Fiona. It appears that your uncle has been murdered."

"Oh my God! Who? When? What happened? He was at the house having lunch just yesterday. Talking and laughing at my dinner table. He was such a good person. I don't understand how this could happen to such a nice man. How could someone kill a *ninety-year-old* man? What is this world coming to when someone kills a sweet old man who plays the role of Santa every year to make children smile? I don't get it. I just don't get it."

Nathan placed a gentle hand on her shoulder in an attempt to calm. "Fiona, I understand how you feel. I really do. I see this stuff every day. We aren't sure yet what went on here. It appears to be an attempted robb'ry. The house was ransacked."

"How...How was he—"

Nathan let out a hesitant sigh. She could see that he didn't want to tell her, but she had to know. Finally, he said, "A neighbor dropped by to see him. There was no response when she knocked on the door, but his car was in the garage, so she called 9-1-1—"

"Annie Jenkins?"

"Sounds like you know her."

"Town crier."

"Well this experience may curb her appetite. He was shot—with his own gun."

Gasping, Fiona cupped her hand over her mouth. Transferring her hands from her face to her chest. In a shaky voice, she managed, "He told us yesterday that he owned a gun." Her eyes suddenly widened as if to scream, aha! "Didn't Uncle Wilbur say that his friend's house was robbed the day before? It must've been Saturday. He said that the robbers took his friend's Santa costume. Remember?"

"I do remember."

Just then the medics pushed open the door to pull a gurney through carrying a black body bag with the words, *ALLEGHENY COUNTY CORONER* printed across it.

Nathan held his hand up. "Hold up a minute, guys. Fiona, I hate to ask you, but we need a family member to ID him. Can you do it?"

Fiona took in a braced breath, and then biting her lip, she nodded. Nathan waved the gurney forward. A medic unzipped the bag only far enough to reveal Wilbur Stacy's head. Squeezing Nathan's hand, Fiona inched her way to the gurney to take a quick look.

"Yes," she whispered. "That's Uncle Wilbur."

Nathan put his arm around her shoulder while the paramedics closed the bag and rolled the gurney away.

"C'mon, I'll drive you home," he said.

"It's really not necessary," Fiona said through a hiccup of tears. "I can walk. It's not far."

"There's no way I'm letting you walk, Fiona. C'mon." Hugging her closer, he led her to his SUV.

Shaking his head, Wyatt turned to Tavia. "Nothing says Merry Christmas like a murder."

"Pfft, *Merry Murder* is more like it."

—⁂—

Even though Fiona expressed that it wasn't necessary, Nathan drove her the block and a half from Guyland Street to Oxford Street. It was yet another warmer than usual day for December. As they made their way to the front door, Nathan noticed something peculiar on the sidewalk. It appeared to be a white powdery substance in a small pile lying at the edge of the cement. He eyed the substance as they passed it, careful not to step on it.

"Thank you for bringing me home, Nathan, but I could've walked. You have an investigation to conduct, and I hate to sound selfish, but I really want you to get on with it," Fiona said, noticing that he was a bit distracted. He kept looking over his shoulder toward the street. For the life of her, she couldn't see what he was so interested in. Oxford Street was completely still.

"Don't worry about a thing, Fiona. I'm on it. I'm so sorry about your uncle. He seemed like a very nice man. Please give my condolences to your family."

"I will, thank you." She took in a fraught breath. "Well, I'd better get to it. There's no easy way to break this news, I'm afraid."

"No, I don't believe there is."

He walked her to the steps of the porch, kissed her on the forehead, then watched as she crossed the porch and entered the house. Upon the door closing, he hurried to the SUV to grab a pair of latex gloves, a plastic evidence bag, and a small brush for collecting suspicious substances. As furtively as possible, he made his way back to the sidewalk, looking for the powdery material. He found it about halfway up the walk. Squatting down, he dabbed his little finger in the tiny pile, smelled it, and then took a taste, spitting it out quickly. Cocaine.

Hastily, he gathered as much of the cocaine as possible from the cement, sweeping it into the bag with the brush. His eyes followed a light trail of the substance that traveled along the very edge of the entire length of the walk. It looked as though it was spilling out of something. Because it was so close to the edge was most likely the reason it hadn't been disturbed.

Cocaine didn't provide a sweet taste. It was a numbing agent that provided a rather bitter taste, therefore, animals weren't so inclined to lick it up. He was thankful for that. He wouldn't have wanted Harriet or the Quinn's Yorkies to ingest the drug. But he had to wonder, who in Fiona's family was using cocaine? Worse, was the drug somehow tied to Uncle Wilbur's death?

He hoped not.

—⚃—

"I just can't believe it," Mom wailed, dabbing her red teary eyes with a cluster of tissues. "Poor Uncle Wilbur. What kind of monster would do such a thing? It's bad enough that they would prey on an old man, but to shoot him with his own gun? How dreadful is that?"

Fiona handed her more tissues. Mom buried her face to weep. The Yorkies, and Harriet, were gathered around her feet as if trying to offer some kind of comfort.

"What does your boyfriend, the detective, think about all of this? Does he have any suspects?" Fiona's dad asked.

"They're just gathering all the on-site evidence now. But as far as I know, they don't have any leads at this time," Fiona said.

"Whoa. You can tell you've got a police officer for a boyfriend. You're using all the *official* lingo," Dad pointed out.

"I've learned quite a bit from Nathan during the past ten months of our dating relationship," Fiona said as she crossed the room toward the Christmas tree. She reached behind to plug it in. "I feel so badly. I've decided that I'm going to leave the tree on twenty-four-seven in Uncle Wilbur's memory in hopes that they find who's responsible for his death before the holidays are over." She no sooner made the commitment when the star blinked once, and then went out.

With heavy hearts, Fiona and her parents stared at the dark star sitting atop the twinkling tree. The sight filled Fiona with a sadness that she'd never felt before. It was almost as if she could feel Evelyn's spirit crying.

"Looks like you're gonna have to replace that star after all, Fiona," Dad said.

"No. It'll come back on. I know it will," Fiona said, with strong conviction

Five

As exhausted as she was, Fiona had spent most of the night tossing in her bed. Terrible scenarios of how her great uncle had been murdered played over and over in her head, as did the vision of his death face looking up at her when they unzipped the body bag for her to identify him. Worse, she was worried about Evelyn. The attic had been completely silent all night. No bumps or creaks throughout the night hours. Her grandmother's presence seemed to have disappeared. The house felt suddenly empty without her.

Finally at five o'clock, she decided that rolling around in the bed was accomplishing nothing more than annoying Harriet, so she decided to get up and do a little kindergarten paperwork that was overdue. She slipped out of the bed, shrugged into her robe, and made her way downstairs. There was no way she could concentrate on paperwork without some coffee. When she flipped on the kitchen light she was stopped in her tracks. There was no coffee in the coffeemaker.

Yep, Mr. Coffee sat silently on the counter—it wasn't popping or gurgling while coffee brewed and trickled into the carafe. Oh, no, it just sat there with the lid up, as it had been left the night before. Evelyn had not made coffee. Since Fiona had purchased the house from her parents, she had never, not once, made coffee in the morning. It was always perked and ready to go when she came down the stairs—whether she was early or not, somehow Evelyn knew to have it ready. The ghostly grandmother even managed to fill the coffeemaker's reservoir with water and place fresh coffee in the basket. Not this morning.

Fiona's heart sank. The Christmas star on the tree was dark. The coffee was not made. Where was Evelyn, and most importantly, would she ever return? A tear ran down her cheek.

—⟐—

"Here ya go, Landry," one of the CSI's said, tossing a file on to Nathan's desk. "Here's the report on the findings at the house on Guyland Street from yesterday. Wasn't that guy supposed to be like ninety years old?"

"Yeah," Nathan replied, while picking up the folder to thumb through the information.

"Found trace amounts of cocaine throughout the house. Mainly in the kitchen, and dining room areas. He had a pair of white gloves on the kitchen table. You know, the kind that all the Santa's wear— those cheap nylon gloves. Anyway, there was traces of cocaine on the fingertips of the right glove, but only the right. The left—clean as a whistle. I realize heroin is the preferred drug nowadays, but isn't this guy a little old to be dabbling in drugs of any kind? He was the Robinson Mall Santa, wasn't he?"

Elbow on his desk, Nathan cradled his forehead in his hand as he read over the report. "Yeah, he was a really nice old guy. I just can't believe he'd have anything to do with drugs."

"Someone said he was your girlfriend's uncle."

"Yep."

"Wow. That's rough. How're ya gonna break the news that her dear old uncle was a junkie?"

Sighing, he tossed the file aside. "I don't even want to think about that right now. Besides, we don't know he was using. We don't have the toxicology report back yet. Although, it won't be any easier to tell Fiona that he was selling cocaine. Hey, I didn't see in the report where you found a Santa suit anywhere in the house."

"Nope. The house was turned up-side-down. They prob'ly got some money, maybe some jewelry. His TV was pretty basic so they left that behind. But no, we didn't find a Santa Claus suit, only the gloves. Do you think they stole his suit?" The CSI seemed rather amazed by the possibility.

"I think they might've." Nathan pushed up from his seat, gathering his jacket from the back.

"Where ya goin'?"

"To talk to the police."

As usual, the traffic on the Fort Pitt Bridge was brutal. Nathan tapped his finger on the steering wheel of his unmarked cruiser. How was he going to broach the subject of the possibility that Fiona's dear old uncle is or was at some time involved with drugs? Then again, he couldn't find any police records involving Wilbur Stacy—just a traffic ticket from 1969. Could Wilbur be a protected witness from years back? Was Great Uncle Wilbur's drug connection a family faux paus that the family never talked about? Skeletons...if there was one thing he'd learned over his ten years on the police force it was every family and every person has them. In fact, he would wager that if he dug deep enough, he would discover that even his sweet little kindergarten teacher, Fiona, had a skeleton or two—certainly nothing too serious, but they'd be rattling around in her closet nonetheless.

Hm...interesting thought. What kind of skeletons could Ms. Fiona Quinn possibly have?

While the traffic inched its way across the bridge closer to the mouth of the Fort Pitt Tunnel, Nathan tried to come up with several scenarios on how to talk to said kindergarten teacher calmly and effectively. He wouldn't be one bit surprised that if the family had a dark secret, Fiona would be completely in the dark about it.

"Fiona...I need to tell you something, and I need for you to stay completely quiet until I finish," Nathan said out loud in rehearsal fashion. "No...that sounds like one of two things: I'm trying to breakup with her or I just told her to shut up and listen—kinda rude." He sighed. He rolled his cruiser forward two car lengths—progress. "Fiona..." He scratched his head. "Fiona...can I ask you a few *delicate* questions about your great uncle? Yeah, right, like—has the old guy ever been arrested for drugs? That ought to keep her calm and open-minded."

Dropping his head against the rest in frustration, he looked to his right. A little old lady with blue hair was throwing him a rude gesture. Had he cut her off? She was mad—he didn't even want to know what she was yelling at him behind the closed window. He let her go in front of him.

He decided to pay attention to the traffic. He was going have to wing it when it came to having the Uncle Wilbur and his drug connection discussion with Fiona. Maybe she'd surprise him. Maybe she'd be very receptive and cool. He knew one thing for sure: he would have to ease into the conversation.

Finally, he had reached the tunnel and the traffic began to flow smoothly. He shook his head. The traffic jams on either side of the Fort Pitt Tunnels was one of the many Pittsburgh mysteries. The cars would jam up for a mile on either side, and then the moment they entered the tunnel they'd drive as if they were out on the open road— it was a mystery he was sure he'd never solve.

—∙∙∙—

"Yeah," Officer Long of the Crafton Police Department began. "I was on that call to the house on Elmdale Street the other day. They tore that poor old guy's house apart. Only thing he said was missing was his Santa Claus suit that he used at the Beaver Valley Mall. He was a seasonal Santa—like the old guy who was murdered on Guyland yesterday."

"And like Mr. Stacy, the only thing they seemed to be interested in was the suit. What's the connection?" Nathan asked, more to himself than to the officer.

"No clue. The man from Elmdale Street was pretty upset. He said there was a good chance he'd be forced to replace the suit. He said that they're responsible for the costumes. They lose them. They replace them. Maybe his home owner's insurance will cover it. I wonder what a Santa suit is worth."

"I'd like to talk to the homeowner, Mr.—"

The officer looked at the file. "Mr. Warner. Yeah, sure, we can drive over and see what he has to say. Maybe he can shed some light on your murder case. Got my doubts."

"Why's that?"

"Seemed a little confused. Might'a been cuz he'd just been burgled, or it might be cuz he watches too much TV."

"Whatta ya mean?"

"He thought we should dust for prints and all that stuff the TV police do. You know how it is. People don't get the difference between TV and reality—even if it's a reality TV show."

"That's true. Well, let's find out what Mr. Warner does know," Nathan said.

Thankfully, the drive from the police department to Mr. Warner's home did not include heavy traffic. The trek wasn't more than five minutes. Usually when thieves burgle a home or business, they are looking for items they can sell quickly in order to get drug money. That's what robberies seemed to be about nowadays—drug money. So what was the interest in the Santa costumes? The costumes had to have a connection, but what could it be?

The house on Elmdale was an older brick ranch. The front porch hadn't been swept in some time. The autumn leaves still huddled in piles in the corners of the rusted metal railings. The outside furniture's cushions were faded and weathered. Crushed beer cans overflowed from a small trash bin. Several tall green oxygen bottles sat just outside the front door.

"You got any leads?" Mr. Warner asked in a raspy voice the moment he opened the door to find Officer Long on his front porch. The pungent smell of cigarettes wafted like a stinky tidal wave through the front door.

"Not at this time, Mr. Warner. This is Detective Landry, homicide. He'd like to ask you a few questions," Officer Long explained.

"What about? No one was murdered here. My house was just robbed." Looking the detective up and down, he scratched his thick grey whiskers.

Nathan stepped forward. "I'd like to ask you a few questions about Wilbur Stacy. I assume that you knew him."

"Yeah, sure, I knew Wilbur. Nice guy. Real good with the kids. Patient, jovial, a real good Santa Claus. Too bad what happened. Although, I'd like to go on record that I never had a problem with ol' Wilbur. I never worked with him either. He worked at Robinson. I worked at Beaver Valley. I took my granddaughter up to see him when she was in town during Thanksgiving. Won't be able to do that next year, I guess." He shot a disgruntled look at Officer Long. "Yinz didn't even check for prints. How 'ya gonna catch this guy if you don't get no prints?"

"What can you tell me about Mr. Stacy? Was he the type to hang out at bars? Did he have a lot of friends?" Nathan asked.

"Like I said, didn't work with him. Didn't hang out with him either. Besides, he was *ninety*. How many ninety year old's do you know who hang out at bars? Most of them are usually in the nursing home, and most of his friends are prob'ly dead. It was all he could manage to play Santa every year, I'm guessin'. Although, he seemed pretty spry. Bet yinz guys dusted for prints at his house, since he was murdered an all. Betcha they left prints here—the burglars, I mean. Yinz outta check. Those police shows on TV check for prints for everything. Don't know why you don't."

Nathan's lips curled. "Ya know, I think he's right, Officer Long. We'd better check the house out. I'm gonna send a crime scene investigator over to take a look around. Would that be okay, Mr. Warner?"

The old guy's face brightened. "Sure. When will he be here?"

"I'll send him as soon as possible. I should be able to get him here sometime this afternoon. In the meantime, please try to keep every-thing as is was. You haven't vacuumed, have you?"

"Not really in the habit of it."

"Good, please don't. Thank you, Mr. Warner. Wish everyone was as cooperative as you." Nathan turned to leave with Officer Long trailing behind.

"You're gonna send a CSI over here? It was a simple burglary. What're you lookin' for?"

"Traces of cocaine. I'll have the CSI dust for a few prints to please Mr. Warner, and I'll see if the two suits are linked by the drugs—win, win."

"C'mon, Detective, if Warner was involved in drugs, he wouldn't want a CSI pokin' around in his house," Officer Long pointed out.

The right side of the detective's lip curled. "Stranger things have happened, Officer Long. Believe me, stranger things have happened."

"We don't own the Santa costumes, Detective Landry," the Robinson Mall manager, explained. "For that matter, we don't hire the Santa's either. We get them through a company near downtown, I believe." She tapped a few keys on the computer at her desk. "Here it is, Characters for All Occasions, they're located on Smallman Street. Mr. Stacy was one of our favorite Santa's, God rest his soul, and we did request him every year, but he was not in our employ—not really."

Twenty-five minutes later, Nathan was standing in front of the storefront for Characters for All Occasions, located in a very popular neighborhood of Pittsburgh known as the Strip District. The Strip is made up of a half-mile square area filled with businesses, boutiques, food markets, restaurants, and nightlife. It is definitely one of the most visited areas of Pittsburgh.

A white van was parked right outside of the character shop with its back doors open. Nathan stepped inside the shop, holding the door open for a man who was exiting in a hurry.

"Thanks, Bob," a woman's voice called out.

"No problem," Bob replied. As he nodded his thanks at Nathan, he dropped a piece of paper. Nathan took it up and handed it to him.

"Thanks," Bob said, stuffing it back into his pocket, and then made his way quickly to the van.

A bell on the door jingled as it dropped closed. The shop reminded Nathan of a Halloween costume store. Only instead of costumes hanging on racks or displayed on mannequins, the perimeter of the large space and the staircase leading to what looked like the office, was filled with life-sized characters and mascots. Large furry animal and famous character's heads sat on shelves in the dimly lit, rather dingy room. Their hollow eyes seemed to follow movement, which gave Nathan the creeps.

He reached into the pocket of his jacket and pulled out a bite size Snickers. He fumbled with the foil wrapper as he eyed the characters. Studying them up close, he was thankful his mother never hired them for any of his childhood birthday parties. He considered clowns creepy, but the characters? Yeah, they were uber creepy. Good call on Mom's part.

The young woman at the counter was wispy thin, with a pierced nose, eyebrow, and lip. Her arms were tattooed, and her hair was dark purple. She was clad in black, including her thick winged eyeliner and lipstick. She looked like she could be one of the characters, or a zombie. She was removing tags from costumes wrapped in long plastic bags on a rack behind the counter when she noticed someone else had entered the shop. Turning, she watched Nathan with hooded eyes as he approached the counter.

"Good afternoon, I'm Detective Nathan Landry, Pittsburgh Homicide," he said around a mouthful of gooey chocolate.

The girl's nostrils flared slightly, making the nose ring jiggle. Her voice was low and expressionless. "Okay."

Nathan pulled out his notepad, dropping his pen. "Oops." He bent down to pick it up. "Clumsy me. I'm here to ask a few questions about Wilbur Stacy, one of your Santa Claus'."

"What about him?"

"Could I ask your name?"

"Nonatha."

Nathan scratched his chin with the pen. "How would ya spell that? Is it No then Natha or would it be Nonatha—one word, or would it be hyphenated, like No hyphen Natha?"

Scowling, her nostrils flared a bit wider—the nose ring now lying flat against it. Her tone was succinct. "It's one word, *Nonatha*."

After writing it down, he held his notepad up to make a big show of examining her name. "Boy that sure is an interesting name. I've never heard that name before, Nonatha, NO-natha, *Nooo* natha." He glanced up to find her glaring at him while rapping her black finger-nails on the counter top. He dug into the jacket pocket to hold up a tiny Snickers wrapped in foil. "Snickers? Their bit size. Perfect for a quick sugar rush." She continued to stare. He cleared his throat. "You gotta last name to go with that?"

The girl sighed, then laconically she replied, "Wilkes. W-i-l-k-e-s, *Wilkes*."

"Nonatha Wilkes, that's easy enough. Thanks."

He leaned against the counter, scanning the room, noticing that someone was watching from a window in the upstairs office. He strolled toward a shelving unit where many oversized heads were stationed, including the Pirate Parrot, George Washington, Abraham Lincoln, and among others, the Steelers mascot, Steely McBeam. He looked them over for a moment, and then plucked George from the third shelf. He turned the smiling first president right then left, examining him closely.

"Don't they use this one at the Pirates games for the pierogi races?"

"Uh-huh."

He tipped the head and slid his own inside, then stretched his arms straight out in front of him to maintain his balance. He staggered in a small circle. "Whoa! I always wondered what it would be like to have one of these on. I don't think I could run a race in this get up. Gives me a little more respect for those who wear mascot costumes." Lifting it off, he expelled a long downward whistle. "Gotta be hot in there too."

"Seriously, I got stuff to do. Was there something you needed, Detective?" Nonatha asked.

Placing George back on the shelf next to Honest Abe, Nathan said, "Oh, yeah, sorry. Got a little carried away. Impressive though, very impressive. I was wondering, what malls in the Pittsburgh area employ your Santa's?"

"Most of them. Monroeville, Robinson, South Hills Village, we've even got two Santa's that cover two shifts at the Beaver Valley Mall."

"What about the Santa costumes? When are they issued to the Santa's, when do they have to return them, and how many Santa's do you employ? I'd like a list, if that isn't too much trouble."

"Um…I'd have to ask my boss. The list of names would be upstairs anyway." She leaned back against the wall, her arms crossed over her tiny chest, glowering at him.

"I see." He waited. She didn't move. He leaned against the counter, studying his shoes. Still, she didn't budge. He said, "Just as a time-saving device, do you think you could ask your boss for that list, like now?"

Nonatha's eyes flicked to the stairs and then back to the detective. Letting out a disgruntled groan, she pushed off the wall to cross the room, and climb the stairs. Her footsteps were heavy with frustration as she ascended, passing Mickey Mouse, Sponge Bob, and Theodore Roosevelt. Creepy—very creepy. She tapped on the door at the top of the stairs and mumbled her request to whoever answered. The door closed. While she waited, Nonatha turned her attention to her cell phone. She tapped at the buttons, read something—most likely a response, and then she tapped out something in return.

Nathan could see several people moving about in the office. They came together in a huddle. He believed they were discussing the request and then the door opened. A rather heavy man surrounded by a plume of blueish smoke came to the top of the staircase.

"I don't just hand out information on my employees. Why do you need a list of our Santa's?" the man asked around the fat cigar sticking out of his face.

"I'm Detective Landry, Pittsburgh Homicide. I'm investigating the murder of Wilbur Stacy, one of your Santa's—"

"None of the Santa's in my employ had a problem with ol' Wilbur, God rest his soul, and most of them didn't even know him. Unless you got a warrant for that list, I'm not giving out any names. You got any leads on Wilbur's murder, Sherlock?"

"Detective Landry—"

"Whatever."

"I'm really not at liberty to discuss an ongoing investigation, Mister—"

"Chezmadia, Jim Chezmadia, and I'm not at liberty to give out the names of my Santa's. Have a nice day." With the slamming of the door, he retreated into the office. The cigar's smoke lingered on the air behind him.

Nonatha stood at the top of the stairs with a poisonous smirk on her black lips. In the young woman's defense, it was the first pleasant expression she'd displayed since Nathan walked through the door.

## Six

Fiona desperately needed a little down time, and when Nathan called to invite her out for pizza, she jumped at the opportunity. She was hoping for a pleasant distraction from Uncle Wilbur's death, six dogs running through the house, and her parents who were not only upset over Uncle Wilbur's murder, but also seemed to be at odds with each other. Not to mention her kindergarten class of holiday hoodlums. Worse, her half-promise to produce Santa Claus at the class's Christmas party tomorrow was going to be broken. Honestly, with everything going on, she'd forgotten all about the party, and now there'd be no Santa Claus for the kids. They would be so disappointed, and she'd be remembered as the worse kindergarten teacher ever.

This wasn't turning out to be the perfect Christmas she'd carefully planned out. Seriously, a murder? Who could've ever planned for that? Who could work around it? Worse yet, Uncle Wilbur's burial was going to be held the morning of Christmas Eve. Blue Christmas would be a grossly poor depiction of this holiday. Maybe horrid holidays, or catastrophic Christmas would be more on point.

The problem with dinner was that Nathan appeared to be distracted. He didn't have much to say. He wasn't making a lot of eye contact. Something was definitely up. Fiona was becoming antsy, and antsy wasn't what she needed at this time. She could be antsy at home or at work, she didn't want to feel that way with Nathan.

"Is something wrong?" Fiona finally asked. "You're miles away. Are you losing interest? Oh, my God. You've met my family and now you're terrified. I don't blame you—especially after my mom kept hinting that we should get married and have children all through lunch yesterday. Don't pay any attention to her. She's just like that.

Honestly, I'm perfectly happy with the way things are. I mean, not that I wouldn't be thrilled if we were to get married—not that I'm saying that we should. What I'm trying to say is I really like you, Nathan, and I don't want anything to ruin that. I dunno, maybe everything I just said might have ruined everything. You do understand what I'm trying to say, don't you—"

"Fiona, I'm not losing interest, and no, your family is not terrifying. Well, maybe a little. All families are terrifying in one way or another. My problem is I need to tell you something, and I just don't know how," Nathan explained.

"Is it bad? It's bad, isn't it? I can tell. It's very bad."

"I don't know for sure how bad it is. It's not good. Can you stay calm about this?"

Fiona straightened her spine against her seat. She adjusted to get more comfortable, or perhaps more braced for whatever he was about to tell her. Folding her hands on the table, she looked him square in the eye, and spoke softly. "I will make every attempt to remain calm. I'm ready. Don't hold back. Give it to me straight."

Nathan took in a deep breath. "When the CSI team was gathering evidence at you uncle's house, they found traces of cocaine in many of the rooms. They did not find his Santa outfit, but the gloves were lying on the kitchen table. The right glove's fingertips had traces of cocaine on them."

Fiona blinked back and then blinked back again. "What does that mean? What are you trying to say? Uncle Wilbur was snorting cocaine? That's just not possible."

"I didn't think so either, but the tests don't lie, Fiona. There was cocaine found in his house, and—"

"There's more? My God, next you're going to tell me there was a meth lab in the basement."

"Thankfully no, but when I took you home Monday after we'd been at Wilbur's house, I found a small pile of cocaine half-way up your sidewalk, and a very light trail that led to your house. Your uncle had been to your house the day before—dressed in his Santa suit. I don't know what to tell you, Fiona, the old guy was in possession of an illegal drug. Who knows why or how, but he was. And perhaps, he was killed because of the drug."

"I don't believe it, Nathan. How many ninety year old men do you know who are involved in a drug ring? Unless they're in the Mafia, and then they're in the ring because they've been in the ring since they were very young, and they can't get out because if they try, the Don or one of his cronies will have him and his family killed or they'll cut off his horse's head, and leave it in the driveway—"

"Bed…They left it in his bed—"

"*Ick*! That's even worse. We're not even Italian, for God's sake."

"Fiona, we're remaining calm, remember?"

She took in a breath. "I'm sorry. Please, continue."

"The toxicology report came in right before I picked you up. It showed that your uncle was not using cocaine. No surprise there. I went to visit your uncle's friend who'd been burgled the day before the luncheon, Mr. Paul Warner. The guy who'd only had his Santa suit stolen? Do you know him?" She shook her head no. He continued, "Anyway, he agreed to let a crime scene tech come look around at his house. I got that report this afternoon—no traces of cocaine found on Mr. Warner's premises. I was hoping there'd be a connection between Mr. Warner's costume and your uncle's, but it doesn't look that way."

"Where do the suits come from? I know that my uncle didn't own his."

"A place on Smallman Street called, Characters for all Occasions. But the owner won't give me a list of his Santas, and unless I can prove there's a connection between your uncle and the other Santas, I can't get a warrant. So far, I've made no connection."

"So that's it? We've hit a brick wall? Now what?" Fiona pressed.

"I'll keep digging."

Fiona flopped her elbows onto the table and dropped her chin into her palms. "Ugh! This is the worst holiday ever. Poor Uncle Wilbur's been murdered, my parents are unhappy, I'm unhappy,

Ev's—er...Um...The dogs are crazy, and to top it off, I've promised the kids a visit from Santa for our Christmas party tomorrow, and obviously, I can't make that happen. Is there any way we can cancel Christmas this year? Or at least order a do-over?"

Snorting, Nathan took her right hand and kissed it. "Other than your uncle's untimely death, things will work out, you'll see. Christmas will be just fine. C'mon, I've got one more thing I'd like to do before I take you home."

—⋙—

"Really? Seriously?" Fiona asked, rather surprised when she found herself in the long line with restless children, in the middle of the Robinson Mall, waiting to visit with Santa. She wasn't exactly sure why she was so surprised. She could never guess what Nathan Landry would do next. Why would sitting on Santa's lap be out of the realm of possibility?

"Aw, c'mon, Fiona. It'll be fun. Your mom will love the photo. She'll have a blast showing it around to all her friends in Florida— her beautiful daughter, the kindergarten teacher, and her dashingly good-looking charming detective boyfriend. Her friends will be so impressed."

"If you say so. Why do I get the feeling there's more to it than that? I mean, this is where my Uncle Wilbur played Santa." She craned her neck to take a look at the Santa sitting in the oversized overstuffed green chair. A little curly-haired girl sporting a fluffy big collared red Christmas dress sat on his lap. "He's not nearly as convincing as Uncle Wilbur. Look at that beard. It's obviously a fake. I think all the mall Santas should be required to grow a beard."

After waiting twenty minutes or so, it was finally Fiona and Nathan's turn to sit on Santa's lap. As they approached the Santa, Nathan and Fiona traded doubtful looks. He was very young. He didn't look a day over thirty. Fiona rolled her eyes. She wasn't at all sure this guy could even grow a beard, if he was required to do so.

The young Saint Nick appeared rather apprehensive when two adults took their places on his knees. Fiona was a little worried the scrawny old, rather young, elf could hold them.

"Ho! Ho! Ho! What can I bring you two lovebirds for Christmas?" he asked.

Nathan opened his jacket to reveal his badge. The Santa's eyes widened in trepidation. Nathan said, "How about a little info, Santa?"

Fiona sighed. Yep, Nathan had ulterior motives for visiting Santa, other than the darling photo for her mother to show off to her girlfriends.

"Look, Buddy, I just started this gig. I don't know nothing about nothing. I'm just trying to earn a little extra cash for the holidays," the Santa said. "And for your information, I didn't know the old guy who had the job before me—the one who was murdered."

"Smile for the camera!" A young girl dressed as an elf called out. Santa, Nathan, and Fiona turned toward her, and smiled. "Thank you. Aw, this is gonna look so cute." She hurried off to prepare the photo for purchase.

"Your costume looks pretty fresh. Did you just pick it up from the dry cleaners?" Nathan asked.

"I got it from the costume company on Smallman Street in the Strip. That's who I actually work for, Characters for All Occasions. I guess the guy who used to do this was really popular. I doesn't matter. I have to have the costume back by six o'clock tomorrow. The mall Santa is only here until five on Christmas Eve. But to answer your question, one of the Santa's told me that they've been collecting the costumes a lot for cleaning. He asked me if they came for mine, but I'm not working for very long—it's the twenty-third for cryin' out loud. Weird. Look, that's all I've got. If you want more information, talk to my boss, Jim Chezmadia. If ya don't mind, I've got a long line of kids waiting." He nodded at the extensive line beyond the gate.

"Thanks," Nathan said.

"No, thank *you*, Officer," Santa handed them each a tiny wrapped candy cane. "Your photo should be ready any minute. You can wait over there."

"Merry Christmas, Santa," Fiona said, as she took Nathan by the hand to lead him away.

"This is what they give out to the kids nowadays?" Nathan complained, while staring down at the miniature candy cane in the palm of his hand. "It's not even a full size cane. Looks like even Santa has downsized."

"Don't worry, they contain enough sugar to pack a real punch. I forbid them in my classroom. Until it's time for bus calls, of course," Fiona said.

"You're not just a cutie. You're a smart little kindergarten teacher, that's for sure."

Blushing, she rolled her eyes.

Fiona was baffled when Nathan drove right past the exit on 376 that would take them to her house in the Westwood neighborhood. Instead, he continued along the highway.

"Where are we going?" she asked.

"I'd like to visit one more Santa this evening. Ross Park Mall is only a little further down the road."

"Wow, you really want my mom to have lots of pictures to show to her friends," Fiona teased.

"You can never have too many pictures of Santa Claus. Besides, I want to see what the Santa at the next mall down has to say."

Fiona shrugged while studying the photo they'd purchased at the Robinson Mall. "I have to admit, we do look totally adorable."

Nathan chuckled. "Was there ever any doubt?"

They were making the announcement that the mall would be closing within the half-hour when Nathan and Fiona took their place on Santa's knees at the Ross Park Mall. Once again, Nathan flashed his badge immediately at the seventy-ish looking man with heavy bags under his eyes. He looked more like a sleep deprived Santa than a merry old elf.

The weary-looking Santa sighed. "Is this about my elf?"

"Your elf?" Nathan asked.

He looked around. When he saw no children in the line, he pulled off his beard. "Yeah, look, I don't know what she's into. I just play Santa. I don't hire the elves, and I don't recommend anyone for the job. So if yinzer here to ask me questions about what went on with your undercover guy, I don't know nothin', and I don't wanna know nothin'."

"Well, you're in luck, Santa, because I don't know what you're talking about. I'm here to ask a few questions about your employer, Characters for All Occasions. Your name is?"

"Pete Robertson," Pete the Santa winced. "Look, since this ain't really Santa request business, do ya mind gettin' up? My knees are killin' me. I'm gettin' the left one replaced in January—had the right one done last June."

Fiona jumped up. "Oh! I'm so sorry! I hope we didn't hurt you."

The old man winked at her. "You can sit on my lap anytime, honey."

Taken aback by Santa's remark, Fiona's mouth dropped open.

Chuckling, Nathan reached into his pocket to pull out a bite-size Snickers. The foil wrapper crinkled loudly as he spoke, "Ya know, I heard that Jim Chezmadia keeps the costumes really clean. You guys turn then in for cleaning quite a bit. I kinda like that. Don't want to get any bugs from a dirty costume. Just sayin'." He tossed the Snickers into his mouth.

"They are fussy this year that's for sure. Didn't used to be that way. We used to get one costume about two weeks before Thanksgiving and that was that. But I don't turn mine in. They come and get it from me right here at the mall and give me a fresh one," Pete said.

"The dry cleaner comes to get it?" Nathan asked.

Pete shrugged. "I dunno who it was. They came in during my break, gave me a fresh jacket, took the old, and off they went."

"So you're not always wearing the same costume?"

"Just the jacket. Funny thing—now that you mention it, Chezmadia bought all new costumes this year. Maybe that's why he's being so picky, but the last costume felt different this costume," Pete noted.

"What do you mean?"

The old guy shrugged. "It was heavier. Like it was weighed down somehow. Not real heavy. I don't ever feel like I'm gonna get a hernia or anything like that—just heavy."

"And this one isn't?" Nathan asked.

He shuffled around as if trying to demonstrate the difference. "Nope, feels normal."

"That's an interesting little fact," Nathan said.

A cool wind had kicked up by the time Nathan drove Fiona home. The moment he opened the SUV's door for her to get out, she immediately noticed that the porch light was not on. Like the coffee in the morning, Evelyn had always put the porch light on for her. Not tonight. She hadn't seen or heard anything from her late grand-mother since the star atop the Christmas tree had gone dark after Uncle Wilbur's death.

"Gee, would've been nice if your parents would've left the light on for you," Nathan said.

"Um, maybe it's burned out. I'll have to check. Looks like they've gone up to bed. Good. That means the dogs will most likely be ken-neled for the night." She let out a relieved sigh.

Nathan stopped mid-way up the walk, staring at the Christmas tree through the picture window. "The star on your tree is out."

"Yeah, I'm not sure that it will ever light again. I hope so."

"Please try not to worry, Fiona. I've got this."

"Do you think that maybe the heavy costumes are carrying some-thing inside?" Fiona asked.

"Like drugs?"

"You said that my uncle may have been killed for the cocaine in his pocket. Could it have been there without his knowing?"

"I suppose so, yes. But I don't know for sure if there is anything in the costumes or if that's just how the costumes feel to that Santa," Nathan pointed out.

"That's true," Fiona agreed.

"We'll find out who killed you uncle. I promise."

"That's a pretty lofty promise, Nathan. Cases go unsolved all the time."

"Not this one." He pulled her close and kissed her lips. "Now get in the house. Looks like December has decided to show up after all."

Fiona went inside, locked the door, flipped the porch light on so Nathan could see his way back to his vehicle. Once he drove away, she climbed the stairs. When she reached the second floor, she noticed a blue light filtering under her parent's bedroom door and heard the muffled chatter from the TV.

She opened her the door just a little and called in, "Goodnight."

"Goodnight," her father replied. "Tell your mom to come upstairs. The dogs are settled in their kennels."

"Mom's not downstairs." She glanced across the hallway to the attic door. Through a slight gap, Fiona could see the stairwell light was on. "I'll get her."

As she past her bedroom, she heard Harriet snoring away—another tiring day for the dogs, she supposed. She made her way up the stairs to find her mother sitting on Grandma's couch. Mom was dressed in her pajamas, robe, and fuzzy pink slippers. Only one lamp was lit, giving the large room a cozy yet lonely atmosphere. "Mom… it's late. What are you doing up here?"

"She's not here, Fiona. I can always feel her presence, but I can't feel her now. I don't know where she's gone, but she *is* gone," Mom said. Her voice was filled with a sadness Fiona hadn't heard since her grandmother's funeral.

Fiona sat down next to her mother and wrapped her arm around her. "Maybe she's gone to visit or to be with Wilbur. After all, he is the last of her siblings to pass-on. Maybe the star going dark on the tree is her way of saying goodbye."

"It was hard enough the first time she said goodbye. Are there any leads in Wilbur's murder?"

"Not so far. But—" Just then something went *click* in Fiona's brain. Her conversation with Nathan over the pepperoni, sausage, and mushroom pizza came booming back inside her head.

*"When I took you home Monday after we'd been at Wilbur's house, I found a small pile of cocaine half-way up your sidewalk and a very light trail that led to your house. Your uncle had been to your house the day before—in his Santa suit. I don't know what to tell you, Fiona, the old guy was in possession of an illegal drug. Who knows why or how, but he was. And perhaps, he was killed because of the drug."*

"Halfway up the walk," Fiona murmured.

"What?" Mom asked, as she lay her head back against the couch.

Fiona didn't hear her. Her mind was on over-drive. She was trying to remember the details of Wilbur's visit before her parents had arrived in Pittsburgh—before she'd gone to the airport to pick them up—before the Sunday luncheon. The problem was so many things had gone on since that visit that the particulars were becoming foggy.

Something in the room went *click*, breaking into Fiona's muse. She looked up to see the old analog TV had turned on. What? The screen was filled with squiggly lines. The TV was buzzing as if it were trying to make some kind of connection. She leaned forward unable to believe what she was seeing, and then the lines cleared, the buzzing silenced, and the old screen began to replay the events of Saturday, December nineteenth—

Incredible! The visit was being reiterated in the form of an old time movie. There she was in the foyer letting Harriet outside, and then she went into the living room, adjusted a bulb on the Christmas tree, and then she swept a branch of the tree aside to look out onto Oxford Street. Wow! There he was—Uncle Wilbur. He walked halfway up the walk and then turned to wave at the neighborhood children who were watching him from their windows. Was that when he spilled the cocaine? Did it somehow drip from the pocket of his Santa coat?

Uncle Wilbur's entire visit was being replayed like an old 'Friends' episode on the TNT cable channel on the aged TV that hadn't been turned on in many years—nor was it hooked up to cable. It was all happening right in front of the couch she and her mother were seated upon. It was mind blowing! Just then the screen showed Uncle Wilbur, dressed in his Santa costume, coming through the front door with Harriet in his arms.

*"Are you in the habit of leaving the front door wide open? Any vaga-bond, like me, could walk right in," Uncle Wilbur said, with a chuckle in his voice, and then he enveloped her in a warm hug.*

*Stepping back to take in his jolly appearance, Fiona said, "Wow. Your costume is very bright this year."*

*"It's brand-spanking new and just had it cleaned. The management from the character company decided that the suites were looking dull, so they gathered them all up the other day, and sent them to the cleaner. Seven days before Christmas. I don't get it. They should've had it done before Thanksgiving." He shook his head. "Can't figure out management nowadays. They don't seem to do anything with common sense in mind."*

*"Tell me about it."*

The screen returned to the squiggly lines, it buzzed for a moment, and then clicked off. After staring at the dark screen for a moment, Fiona glanced around the apartment. Was there anything else Evelyn was trying to show her? She had to wonder if Evelyn were trying to show her something she'd missed. Did this mean that her grand-mother had returned? She glanced across the couch to see if her mother had witnessed the amazing TV vision. Evidently not. She was asleep.

"The suit had just been returned to him, because it had just been cleaned," Fiona said out loud, although she didn't realize that she had.

"What? What did you say?" Mom asked.

Fiona shook her head. Her mother had pulled her out of her funk. "Nothing, Mom, just talking to myself."

"They have doctors for that sort of thing, ya know," Mom said around a sleepy yawn.

Fiona chuckled. Taking her mother's hand, she said, "C'mon, we'd better get to bed."

Uncle Wilbur's words repeated over and over in Fiona's head while she dressed into her pajamas, and they wouldn't be silenced as she lie awake staring into the darkness. *"Just had it cleaned...Just had it cleaned."* Maybe that was the connection Nathan was looking for. She was certain that Evelyn wanted her to remember the conversation she had with Wilbur and that's why her grandmother provided such a vivid recollection of his visit—on the old analog TV. If Evelyn knew what had happened to her brother, why didn't she just come right out and tell her somehow?

The fact was Evelyn was trying to tell her—in her ghostly way.

The TV was the only tool available to Evelyn. Hey, she used to make coffee. Why couldn't she turn on a TV?

Regardless, Fiona had to go with what she knew—all the Santa costumes had just been cleaned. But what dry cleaners did the character company use? There were several dry cleaners in the downtown area—and because of the close proximity, one would think they would use one of those, but the downtown dry cleaner's would most likely cater to business suits, slacks, dress shirts, and quick touch ups for spur-of-the-moment business meetings. A costume company would need a more heavy-duty cleaner. Someone who could handle bigger more complicated cleanings. Like...Three Brothers Dry Cleaning in Robinson Township—not too far from downtown.

She rolled over to look at the clock for the hundredth time—two o'clock. Lying in bed was pointless. She simply could not sleep, and she found herself having a crazy thought—maybe she should drive to Robinson Township and check out Keith Schlemmer's dry cleaners. No, she didn't plan to break into the business—that would be criminal and truly crazy. She'd lose her job, and like most people, she needed a paycheck. But what if she merely checked out their dumpster situation? She was fairly sure that wasn't against the law. Well maybe trespassing was, but she hardly believed they could throw you in jail for trespassing in a dumpster—hopefully.

Perhaps someone left something behind in the trash that would give her some kind of a clue as to why her uncle and the other Santa's house was broken into or what the thieves were looking for. A good clue wasn't a strong possibility, but any clue at all would do—if she was even shrewd enough to recognize a good clue. After all, she had no idea if the dry cleaner was involved, but hey, it was worth a look, right?

*C'mon, Fiona, quit being such a sissy. You've got to do this for Uncle Wilbur. He can't go to his grave in disgrace—not on your watch.*

Decision made.

## Seven

Everyone was sleeping. Sneaking out of the house shouldn't have been too much of a problem. Fiona was confident she didn't have to worry about Harriet giving her away. The little Maltese was down for the count. She was snoring so loudly from underneath the blankets that no matter where Grandma Evelyn had gone to, Fiona was sure she could hear the noise.

Within five minutes or so, Fiona was as ready as she possibly could be. She'd pulled on a black turtleneck, black jeans, and black boots. From all the TV shows and movies she'd seen over her lifetime that seemed to be the proper attire for one who did not want to be detected. Right?

By moonlight, she took another look in the mirror to make sure the black face paint she'd applied from a jar she'd bought for a Steeler's party last fall was staying on. She was fairly sure her face was black enough, although she wasn't quite sure how black it was supposed to be. Fiona was not accustomed at all to being somewhere she wasn't supposed to be or doing something she wasn't supposed to do. She was a rule-follower, a do-gooder—Hokay, except for that one little slip-up at Mrs. Adams's home years ago. Nowadays, her stomach twisted at the very thought of doing anything underhanded. Although, she wasn't sure what she was about to do could be construed as wrong or dishonest, but she had a feeling that it could be considered, at the very least, trespassing. She could hear the headlines on the KDKA morning newscast: Local kindergarten teacher arrested for dumpster diving—details after the break. And those details could possibly include her firing. Not good.

She took in a calming breath. Well, it wasn't exactly doing the trick at calming her, but at least she was getting some oxygen to her brain.

Closing her eyes, Fiona repeated to herself, *I'm doing this for Evelyn. I'm doing this for Wilbur. I'm doing this for Evelyn. I'm doing this for Wilbur.* The mantra wasn't helping to quell her rising anxiety, but it was succeeding in reminding her of the objective: prove Uncle Wilbur innocent of any wrong doing before his burial. With that in mind, she eased out of her bedroom, closing the door on the eight pound Maltese, still sawing logs louder than any lumberjack could compete with.

Fiona tiptoed past her parent's room, hoping not to alert the Yorkies of her presence, which was a major victory—the floors in the hallway creaked terribly. She descended the staircase furtively, step by step, as it was as notorious for creaks and squeaks as the hall was.

The soft glow illuminating the foyer from the twinkle lights on the tree reminded her of many Christmas mornings. She and Chad would creep down the stairs to see if Santa had visited and then they would scurry back upstairs to wake their poor exhausted parents, alerting them that Santa had arrived! She smiled at the memory.

At last she made it to the foyer. She was home free. Letting out the breath she'd been holding, she crossed to the front door. She laid her hand on the doorknob—

"Where on Earth are you going at this time of night?" Her mother's voice boomed through the twinkle.

Fiona jumped a good two feet in the air. She turned to find her mother sitting on the couch in the soft light. "Mom...what are you doing up?"

The lamp next to the couch came on. There she was, in her jammies, a cup of tea in hand, with one of the Yorkies draped over her lap and her head tilted to the right. She was looking at Fiona as if she was a rebellious teenage girl, sneaking out of the house to meet a boy who her parents vehemently disapproved of—which never happened, by-the-way.

Mom replied, "I couldn't sleep. Where are you going, and what's that stuff all over your face?"

"I...I...couldn't sleep, so I thought I'd—" Fiona expelled a vanquished sigh. "Oh, I can't lie to you. Never could, not that I ever really had a mind to lie to you—except for that whole Mrs. Adams fiasco that Chad felt so necessary to bring up at lunch. He can be such a little—" She let out another sigh. "Anyway, beyond that there really was never anything to lie about. I was too busy with school-work and dance classes to get into trouble, so it's not like I had to make up stories to get myself out of any kind of trouble—"

"Like now?"

"I'm not in trouble."

"Then why are you sneaking out of the house at two in morning with whatever that is on your face? Are you going to rob a jewelry store?"

"What? No! Why would you ask me that?"

"You look like a cat burglar. Isn't that what cat burglars do, rob jewelry stores?"

"I—I don't know."

"What then?"

It was over. She'd been caught—before she'd even walked out of the house. Maybe it was all for the best. At least she wouldn't be the lead story on the morning news, and she wouldn't lose her job. Still, she felt the need to prove that Uncle Wilbur was innocent. If not her, then who? Nathan had to work under strict perimeters—ethics, murder police rules, and all the other red tape involved that she knew nothing about. The investigation would be slow going. Poor Uncle Wilbur would be buried Thursday morning with a shadow of shame cast over his reputation. She couldn't let that happen. Not to Uncle Wilbur. Not to Santa Claus. Yes, Lincoln Parrish, there was a Santa Claus—his name was Wilbur Stacy.

"Fiona…tell me what's going on," Mom pressed.

Feeling defeated, Fiona plopped a heavy shoulder against the wall. "I had a plan. A really stupid plan to prove that Uncle Wilbur was not involved with drugs or a drug cartel."

"*What?* What are you talking about?"

The proverbial cat had just leapt right out of the proverbial bag. Fiona proceeded to explain to her mother about the cocaine that had been found in Uncle Wilbur's house, and on her very own sidewalk after his visit. She also reiterated how Wilbur's suit had just been cleaned as had the rest of the Santa costumes. Mom listened to the entire story with wide eyes and raised eyebrow interest.

"This is ridiculous," Mom stated. "There's been some kind of misunderstanding. You mentioned that you have a plan. Well, I'm listening."

"I think the answers might lie at the dry cleaners. And I think with a little snooping, I might be able to come up with at least a little evidence to swing the investigation in their direction."

"What kind of evidence?"

"That I don't know, but I'm willing to go dumpster diving to hopefully find out."

Setting her tea on the coffee table, Mom pushed to her feet. "I'm in."

"What?"

"You heard me. I'm in. Let me get in some dark clothing, and we'll do this."

"Mom...you can't be serious."

"Why not? I've done some pretty crazy things in my day. I was a wild child of the seventies, and some of that wildness spilled over into the eighties, too. I mean, I had to get it all out of my system before getting married and having children. Let's see...there was the streaking incident at Three Rivers Stadium in seventy-nine. Honestly, I can't recall what went on at the Rick James concert in eighty, but now I'm wondering if I'm his super freak—"

Fiona flipped her hands up in halting motion. "O-M-G! Too much information!"

Mom chuckled. "Give me five minutes. I'll be right down." On her way to the stairs, she dropped the dog in Fiona's arms—it was Keith.

Fiona could only manage a stymied, "Um—"

"Oh, quit being such a stick-in-the-mud, Fiona Nicole, and go get that jar of face paint."

—m—

She couldn't believe it. Fiona simply could not believe that she was driving along Steubenville Pike at two-thirty in the morning with her mother to go dumpster diving. She could have never predicted this turn of events, that's for sure. She also couldn't believe her mother insisted on bringing Keith.

"If I try to put him in his kennel, I'll wake the other dogs, and the yipping will begin. We'll wake up your father. Do you want that?" Her mother said in self-defense.

She had a point, or was it that Fiona didn't have another choice? Anyway, there they were driving toward the Three Brothers Dry Cleaning in the wee hours of the morning. The roads were practically empty, only a car here or there. Still, Fiona's stomach was twisting and grinding like they had a dead body in the trunk that they intended on dumping in the dry cleaner's trash. How silly. What they were about to do wasn't a big crime, like murder, robbery, or kidnapping. Fiona was spending a lot of mental time trying to convince herself that dumpster diving wasn't a crime at all. It would be trash—in a dumpster. The trash was probably considered public domain for all she knew. At least she could hope.

Fiona sighed. What was she looking for once she got into the dumpster? Anything—everything, she supposed. It sure would be nice, or at the very least convenient, to have even the vaguest idea before climbing into the filth. She shuddered. How dirty could a dry cleaner's dumpster be? It was a dry cleaner—they cleaned things. Maybe their trash was clean too—again, wishful thinking or hoping on her part. Worrying about the trash didn't really matter. She was about to find out.

She glanced at her mom in the passenger seat. Her lips curled. Her mom looked like an intrepid soul with her face slathered in black paint. Who knew? She also appeared quite calm about what they were about to do. She casually gazed out the window with Keith on her lap, stroking his ears. Hmmm, maybe she really was a wild child back in the seventies. Fiona wasn't sure if she should be proud or terrified of her mother.

Fiona always thought of her mother as Carol Brady of the *Brady Bunch*—at least that's the persona her mother projected for her and her brother. *Well played, Mom, well played.* Now with the 'wild child' information her mother confessed to, she would have to readjust her assessment of mom. Maybe mom was more like Peg Bundy of *Married with Children*.

So where did that leave her dad? Was he Mike Brady, Al Bundy, or the professor from *Gilligan's Island*? Whatta a weird thing to come to mind. She shook the thought from her head.

Whether dumpster diving was a misdemeanor or not, they needed to be quiet about it. She wasn't so sure that would be accomplished. Would the dog stay in the Mini Cooper without yipping? She had serious concerns.

Fiona also wasn't sure if her mother had made the link between the Three Brothers Dry Cleaning and Keith Schlemmer. The day he dropped by the house with Keith, the dog, in hand, she appeared more absorbed by his presence than anything he had to say. Well, blood is usually thicker than water, so if Keith's dry cleaner raises any suspicions that he is connected to Wilbur's murder in any way, she may not be so charmed by her ex-lover—ouch! There was *that* image again. She was quick to dismiss that thought by the sight of the entrance to the parking lot of the dry cleaner just beyond the upcoming intersection.

She rolled the Mini Cooper to a stop at the light. A car pulled up next to her. Suddenly, Fiona could feel eyes upon her. She turned to find an older man staring at her. His eyebrows were furrowed. He gripped his steering wheel tightly.

*What's his problem?* Fiona thought to herself.

He quickly turned away. His reaction to her gaze made her realize how scary she must look at two-thirty in the morning with her face painted. The light turned green. Thankfully, he turned left, while she continued straight toward the parking lot to her right.

Ready or not—it was go time.

"Three Brothers Dry Cleaning—isn't that what Keith Schlemmer said the name of his business was?" Mom inquired, her voice was a little on the high-pitched side for Fiona's liking.

"It is."

"I can't believe that—" Stopping mid-sentence, Mom let out a disenchanted sigh. She was silent as they made the turn into the lot. As if she'd shook off any reliability of character toward her former fiancé, she said, "The dumpster should be around back, I'd imagine."

Turning her headlights down to parking lights, Fiona steered the car around the side of the brick building. Down a short thruway a large bright red *NO TRESSPASSING* sign greeted them. Fiona hit the brake. She exchanged a hesitant glance with her mother.

"Well, what's it gonna be?" Mom asked with one eyebrow arched.

Biting her lip, Fiona pressed the accelerator pedal to move forward down the alley. Fat sinewy bushes of some sort that had shed their foliage lined the narrow alley. As they rounded the back corner of the building the dumpsters came into view—two of them, which was more than she had expected. They were located just outside a back door under a dusk to dawn light. It wasn't very bright. Fiona figured the low lighting would be in their favor.

She parked the car just beyond the dumpsters. She and her mother sat quietly for a moment or two taking in the area which was a small paved lot that butted up to a convenience store, which also had two very large dumpsters. The area with the dumpsters from the dry cleaners and other stores that shared their lot was corralled by a chain linked fence. A no trespassing sign was attached to the fence—in case you didn't see the first one at the beginning for the alley, Fiona supposed.

"Well, if we're going to do this, we should get moving," Mom whispered.

"There's a flashlight in the glove box," Fiona whispered back, although she wasn't exactly sure why they were whispering. There was no one about, and they were still inside the car. "How much garbage do you think is inside the dumpsters?"

"I don't know. It depends on when the last trash pickup was, I'm guessing. That said, we want trash don't we? I mean, if the dumpsters are empty what good would that do us?"

"Right, right. You're right, of course." Fiona took in a steadying breath, and then blew it away. "Okay…let's do this."

"*You're* doing this—I'm the lookout. I'm way too old for dumpster diving, my dear. I was the wild child of the seventies—not the millennium," Mom said.

Fiona rolled her eyes.

They eased out of the car, leaving Keith behind. Ears perked, tongue hanging out, he watched out the driver's side window, but he remained quiet. Fiona was impressed and relieved. They crept toward the first dumpster only to be quite surprised at how high it actually was. Mom took one side of the lid, while Fiona took the other and on their tippy toes they pushed it open. They stood back, considering their options and the smell. Well, Fiona's question about the cleanliness of the dry cleaner's dumpster had just been answered. Ick!

"I don't think I can jump all the way up there. How am I going to get in?" Fiona asked.

Fiona's mom bent over slightly with her hands together, palms up, fingers braided. "Use my hands as a stepstool. I'll give you a little bump up."

Considering it the best, if not the only reasonable option, Fiona gingerly placed her right foot in her mother's hands, and stretched to grab the top of the dumpster. "I'm going to need more than one shower after this," she grumbled.

"Are you ready? Here comes the hoist!" Mom jerked her hands upward, while Fiona hopped toward the ridge of the can. She dangled over the edge for a moment teetering on her hips, looking downward into the blackness of the large trash bin, holding her breath, while praying that when she jumped in there wouldn't be any rats. Double ick!

Mustering all the courage she could find, Fiona lifted her right leg over the top, then jumped into the dumpster, landing on bags and bags of garbage. Something in the bag under her derriere went *squish*. Feverishly, she pulled the flashlight from her hip pocket. With her thumb, she fumbled with the switch in a panic for light, while trying to fight back a strong urge to retch. The smell of rotted food and other unidentifiable stench was overwhelming in the deep dark confined space. She considered trying to hold her breath, but then realized that wouldn't work—not for the amount of time she'd be required to remain in the dumpster. Most likely she'd pass out, and the thought of lying in a filthy dumpster unconscious with bugs crawling over her was more than she could bear. She decided to try breathing through her mouth. As quickly as possible, she yanked a pair of latex gloves from the other pocket and slipped them on.

"Are you okay?" Mom called.

"Yeah," Fiona said, hesitating at the soft echo from her own voice inside the can. Her lip wrinkled in derision. She set straight to work, looking for anything that just might connect the dry cleaners to the Santa's or to Wilbur or with any luck at all, both.

This was going to take longer than she originally thought. Funny, when she watched the CSI programs on TV, they seemed to discover something evidence-worthy within the first few bags. Fiona wasn't finding that to be the case. She was opening bag after bag containing discarded fast food, napkins, plastic bags filled with more fast food and napkins, and much to her disgust, some personal hygiene products. Gross!

She was happy that she remembered to bring latex gloves, and actually she was moving through the bags quite quickly. It wasn't like she wanted to linger inside the dumpster, that was for sure, but it was looking like she'd have to dive into the second dumpster—nothing was panning out in this one.

Finally, she opened the last bag. Her flashlight illuminated a bunch of papers—all crinkled up tightly. One by one she unwrinkled them to see what was written or typed or copied onto them. At last, at the very bottom of the bag, she came to a small note.

"Fiona—"Mom called in a high-pitched whisper.

The note was crumpled tightly. Her fingers weren't working so well under the latex. The paper was sticking to the gloves.

"Fiona—"Mom's voice grew a little more intense. She knocked on the dumpster as if it were a door.

Finally, the little yellow note was open. She shined the flashlight on it.

Mom's voice was filled with total panic. "Fiona! Someone's coming!"

The note was a list. But part of the note was missing. It had been ripped in half. She rifled through the bag to see if the other half was stuck at the bottom.

"Fiona—there's headlights coming around the building. We've got to get out of here!"

There it was—the other half of the note. Holding the flashlight in the crook of her neck, she put the two pieces together. It was a list alright, and it may very well be what they were looking for. Just then the top of the dumpster became very bright. A siren sang out, and then just as quickly shut down. The lights swirling overhead were blue and red and white.

Groaning, Fiona stilled. It was the police.

Quickly, she stuffed the two pieces of the note into her bra. She climbed the stack of bags to peek out of the dumpster just in time to see two police officers get out of their cruiser, and walk toward her mother, who had her hands up. The police didn't have their guns drawn—only flashlights in hand. What was her mother doing? From inside the Mini Cooper, Keith was barking like a Doberman, while trying to wiggle through the gap Mom had left in the window for air.

A second flashlight turned on, beaming directly into Fiona's eyes. She couldn't see her, but the voice of Tavia Andrews was most familiar.

Obviously baffled, Tavia asked, "*Fiona*…is that you?"

Just then Keith managed to free himself from the confines of the Mini Cooper. Growling, he dashed across the paved lot to bite the officer who was standing next to Tavia on the ankle!

Fiona groaned. *Perfect. Just perfect.*

## Eight

How much worse could this holiday get? Chevy Chase's Christmas movies were starting to look like a painting by Currier and Ives in comparison to how Fiona's holiday was turning out. On top of everything else, she and her mother were now sitting in a holding cell at the Allegheny County Police Department with a rough-looking woman dressed like an elf.

The woman was wearing way too much makeup. Her hair was neon pink, and her elf costume was not only too tight, but not at all appropriate for being out in public. She sat on a bench across from Fiona, her mother, and Keith, staring at them while popping her gum. She said her name was Bunny, but Fiona didn't believe her—it was some kind of alias, no doubt.

"Why're ya wearin' that black crap all over your faces? Yinz rob a jewelry store or somethin'?" Bunny asked at one point. Then she leaned forward to take a big whiff of Fiona. Grimacing, she pinched her nostrils closed with her fingers. "A very stinky jewelry store."

Mom turned to her daughter. "See? I told you that you looked like a cat burglar."

Fiona expelled a frustrated breath. "Yes, Mother, you did mention something like that."

Just then the door opened. Tavia walked through with Nathan right behind her. He looked rather disgruntled. Fiona didn't blame him. This was the moment she'd dreaded the most. She was probably going to lose her job *and* her boyfriend.

*Dumpster diving—great plan, Fiona, great plan. Idiot.*

"Sorry about this, Nathan. Some old guy called it in, and if I hadn't had my partner along I would've just let them go. But you know how Frank is—everything by the book. Of course it didn't help that the dog bit him. Good thing his wife went into labor, or he would've put them on the books, that's for sure," Tavia explained as they approached the cell. She unlocked the cell door, then opened it up. Fiona was amazed—the cell doors really do squeak as they swing open—just like on TV. Tavia and Nathan entered the cell.

"Hello, Mrs. Quinn. It's nice to see you again," Nathan said with a pleasant smile on his lips.

"I don't know what got into Keith," Mom began. "He must've thought I was in some kind of danger and was trying to protect me. You can't blame him for that, can you? I mean, they won't put him down or anything, will they?"

Tavia said, "I think your dog is safe, Mrs. Quinn. He's got all his shots, and I convinced the officer that he didn't really want to admit to the other officers that he'd been taken down by a Yorkie—if he'd been a bigger dog, I'm not sure my argument would've been as convincing. Besides, it wasn't a bad bite—it was more of a nip. By the way, Fiona, please note that dumpster diving, in general, is not against the law—unless there are no trespassing signs in place. Not only were there signs, but the area was fenced in, indicating the business did not welcome dumpster divers. Honestly, I never had you pegged—"

"Looks like we owe you a world of thanks, Officer Andrews. I'll be buying coffee for months," Nathan said. Tavia shot him an ornery grin backed up with a nod.

He turned to Fiona. At that moment the stench of garbage must've wafted in his direction—his nose crinkled while his face contorted in a most unpleasant manner. He managed, "Hello Ms. Quinn, it's always a pleasure to see your lovely face. Although I think you may be wearing just a little too much makeup this evening." He swatted at the smell that was assaulting his nose. "I'm not sure what that perfume is you're wearing, but you might want to pitch it when you get home." Fiona attempted to speak. He put his hand up. "Not a word."

Shrinking in her seat, Fiona bit her lip. She felt as though she was reliving the whole Mrs. Adams and the broken window debacle all over again, and she hated it.

*Idiot.*

Nathan said, "Thank you Officer Andrews, I'll take it from here. And I'll have that latte that you like so much on your desk tomorrow." He wiggled his forefinger at the two black-faced prisoners to follow him from the cell. Before he stepped out, he turned to the woman dressed as a cheap elf, and said, "Hi Bunny, how've ya been?"

"Hey, Nate, good. Yourself?"

"Can't complain. I see you're back to your old tricks."

She laughed. "It's all about keepin' life interesting."

"Kind of like someone else I know. You take care now, Bunny. Ya hear?"

They made their way down the hall and out the door into the main room.

"How do you know *her*?" Fiona asked.

"Everybody knows Bunny."

"And for your information, Detective Landry, I am not up to any *old tricks*. And I don't believe for one moment that *anyone's* name is really Bunny."

Suppressing a chuckle, Nathan turned to Tavia. "Again, thanks for keepin' them off the books, Tav."

"Well, it's not all good news. Frank was in the process of having her car impounded before he was called away, but I managed to intercept—a little. They towed it to her house."

Fiona winced. "Does my dad know?"

Tavia shrugged. "Sorry."

Nathan said, "C'mon, I'm taking you two…*Cat burglars* home, and on the way, you've got some serious explaining to do."

Fiona's mother pitched her yet another *see, I was right* look. Fiona rolled her eyes. The last thing the wild child of the seventies needed was affirmation.

They hadn't driven twenty feet down the street from the station when Nathan inquired in an expectant voice, "*Well?*"

"Well…" Fiona dug down the front of her turtleneck sweater into her bra to produce the two ripped pieces of paper. "I found this. I don't know for sure what it is, or if it's at all helpful, but it's all I had time to come up with. I'm sorry if I've upset you, Nathan, but I felt I had to do something. Not that I think that you're not doing anything, of course you are, but I know that you can't just go into any ol' dumpster looking for evidence—"

"Actually, neither can you, Fiona." He pulled the SUV into a nearby parking lot.

"I know what I did was daring—"

"And against the law." He turned on the cab lights to see what was on the papers.

She groaned. "I'm sorry. I just—"

"Hold the phone. You just may have found something that I can work with," Nathan said. Fiona's mother moved forward to look over his shoulder. He continued, "You were right. This is a list, and it looks like it's a list of Santa's with some kind of number code." He turned to Fiona. "I think it's pretty impressive that you recognized it as something to gather up."

He held the note out for Fiona and her mother to see.

SN-200-A
SN-933-E
SN-570-A
SN-1000-E
Sn-100-A
SN-301-E

"I can see how you're coming up with the fact that it looks like a code, but how do you know it has anything to do with Wilbur or the Santa's?" Mom asked. "And yes, how did you know it was relevant, Fiona?"

"I didn't. Remember, I was looking for *anything*. I could see that this was obviously a list, but I didn't know if it was pertinent. It was the only thing, other than actual garbage, that I came up with. Looking at it more closely now, the S and the N could stand for Saint Nick, but I have no idea what the numbers mean or the letter after the numbers. I bet this is really simple, too. Once we figure out what the number stands for, I bet we'll be totally amazed at how simple the code actually is."

"But how will you figure out what the numbers mean?" Mom asked.

"Give me your notepad, Nathan," Fiona said. He dug in his pocket and gave it to her. She set straight to copying down the list, and then tore the paper off the pad. "Guess we'll have to put on our thinking caps."

"Said the kindergarten teacher," Nathan said, with a chuckle in his voice.

—✖—

Fiona couldn't wait to take a shower. She felt beyond dirty, and the face paint was starting to itch. When they arrived home, her father was waiting for them in the living room, and he wasn't happy that he'd been awakened by the tow truck driver, rapping on the front door. He was even less happy to hear that she and her mother had been in the lockup.

Much to Fiona's delight, and surprise, her mother stepped forward to handle her father, who was shooting questions at them as fast as an automatic rifle. Her mother, God bless her, jumped in to answer all his questions in a calm cool manner. With a hitch of her chin, she signaled Fiona to go upstairs.

As good as the hot water felt and how nice it was to be rid of crawling garbage sensation, Fiona didn't linger in the spray. The scribbled note with the numbers and letters she'd hurried to copy from the ripped paper were niggling at her. SN—then a three-digit number, except for one—it had four digits, yet they all had the letter A or the letter E following the number. SN…could possibly stand for Saturday night or Sunday night. No, it had to stand for Saint Nick, but what about the rest? What could they represent? Maybe nothing at all. Maybe it was just an insignificant list of who knows what?

After getting into her cozy pajamas, and fighting her way around Harriet to get into the bed—the little dog had a real knack for taking up most of the bed, and she was always dead center. Fiona took one more look at the note before turning out the light to try to get at least an hour or two of sleep before facing her kindergartners, and the Santa-less Christmas party.

She lay staring at the ceiling. Rolling over and over, she stared at the wall, the alarm clock, the window, and then back to the ceiling. Still, she couldn't close her eyes, nor her mind. What did the numbers signify? Lying in bed was futile. She could not close her eyes, let alone sleep. She got out of the bed, leaving Harriet to stretch out all the more.

Taking the note with her, Fiona went into the computer room at the end of the hall and turned on her PC. The screen projected a blue hue through the room as she sat staring at the Google home page, trying to figure what to ask the all-knowing search engine.

Lost for a solid request, she typed: *The Mall at Robinson, Pittsburgh, Pa.* Lists instantly appeared on the screen, including the mall's address, a Wikipedia description, list of restaurants at the mall, the mall's Facebook page link, and the retailers located at the mall. She looked at the note lying next to the computer. *Hmmm.* She typed in: *Monroeville Mall—200 Mall Circle Drive; South Hills Village—301 South Hills Village; Waterworks—933 Freeport Road; Station Square, and even Beaver Valley Mall0—570 Beaver Valley Mall Boulevard.* The corners of her lips lifted—the pieces to the puzzle had fallen into place.

"Fiona," her mother whispered from behind her chair. "I think you just found the answer."

"Couldn't sleep either?"

"No, your list was keeping me up," her mom confessed.

"I think you're right. I think I've cracked the little code," Fiona said, while scrubbing her palms together triumphantly.

"Um…I was thinking, you do realize that there was something we didn't tell Nathan," Mom said.

"You mean the fact that we know Keith Schlemmer? We were so wrapped up in getting caught by the police, and the note, I completely forgot." Turning off the screen, she pushed to her feet.

"Where are you going?"

"To bed. I can get about an hour and a half before I have to go to school, and I sure could use it. Well, that's if Harriet will let me into the bed. I might have better luck on the couch."

"Aren't you going to call Nathan?"

"I'm sure he's sleeping by now. He needs his rest as much, if not more, than we do. I'll call him first thing in the morning."

## Nine

"I'm ready," Mom announced, when Fiona stepped into the kitchen with dark circles under her eyes.

Fiona was too exhausted to deal with any more wild escapades, but she dared to ask, "Ready for what?"

Her mom poured coffee into two travel mugs. "To go to school with you this morning. I'm going to help you with your Christmas party." She handed Fiona a mug.

With a hesitant yet anticipative tone to her voice, Fiona asked, "Did Evelyn make this?"

"No, sweetheart. I'm afraid I did, sorry."

Fiona's shoulders slumped in disappointment. "Wishful thinking, I suppose. Anyway, why would you feel the need to help me with my job?"

"I don't *need* to—I *want* to. It's not like I don't have experience. I'm a retired teacher for crying out loud. Besides, it'll get me out of the house for a few hours. I think it'll be fun to see the kids so excited for Christmas and to watch you interact with them. It'll give me a feel for what it'll be like with grandchildren—"

Fiona let out a very loud sigh, while pitching her mother a baleful look.

Mom expelled an evil chortle. "Okay, okay, you can't blame a wannabe for trying. Anyway, I can help serve the cookies and punch or help with a craft. You do have a craft planned, don't you?"

"I'm a kindergarten teacher, Mom. My whole life revolves around crafts." Fiona took a sip of the coffee.

A sound something similar to a tiny buffalo herd thundering toward them roared from the foyer. Fiona and her mom turned to see a mob of Yorkies coming into the kitchen—Harriet was not among the horde. A few seconds later Fiona's dad followed. He carried the old Christmas star in his right hand and a screwdriver in the left.

"Good thing I filled the doggie dishes," Mom said, counting the Yorkies as they past. "Oh, for crying out loud, Garrett! Where's Keith?"

He plopped a sleepy kiss on her cheek as he made his way to the coffeemaker. "He's still sleeping in his kennel. I guess a night in the slammer was exhausting for the little guy. How are my two jailbirds this morning?"

Giggling, Mom bent down to pat the dog's heads, and then said, "I'm going to school with Fiona. I'll be ready to go in just one minute." Tossing Fiona's dad a wink, she left the kitchen.

Peeking over her coffee mug, Fiona asked, "Are...are you upset with me, Dad?"

He stilled, mid-pour of his coffee. Turning toward her, Fiona's dad asked, "Upset about what?"

"Getting in trouble with the law last night. I mean, I've never gotten into trouble before, with the actual law—the police, I mean. We probably wouldn't have got caught if that old man hadn't seen our painted-up faces at the stoplight. I know that's who reported us. But I had to do what I had to do. Not that I don't think that Nathan is perfectly capable—of course he is. I guess I got impatient. Sometimes I do that, not with my class, never with the children. I'm a good teacher. I just get impatient with things like—"

"Fiona...you are a grown woman. You make your own decisions. You don't need your daddy's approval." He kissed her on the forehead. "I'm proud of ya, baby. Even if you are an ex-con."

Fiona tossed her head back in laughter. "Oh, Dad, I didn't even get finger printed, let alone booked. I was lucky, and I don't think I'll be breaking any laws ever again. Well, any time soon anyway—at least I hope not. Change of subject—what are you doing with grandma's star?"

"It's still not lighting, so I thought I'd take a look. I think there may be a broken wire since we replaced all the tiny bulbs and it still won't light. I'll take it apart and check it out. But remember, it's old—it may just be plain used up."

"I have every confidence that you'll get it fixed." She started for the foyer but then turned back. "Oh! Today is trash pickup day—after being so intimate with a dumpster, how could I forget that?"

"Don't worry, I'll see to it that the trash gets to the curb."

"Thanks, Dad."

"C'mon Fiona, we'll be late for school," her mom called from the foyer.

Hokay, *now* it seemed just like old times.

The light breeze from yesterday had turned to a brisk wind with a sneaky snowflake tucked in every now and then. Thusly, Fiona decided it was a good idea to drive—especially with her mom along for the day. As she steered the car down Oxford Street for the two minute drive to school, she said, "Dad seems to be in a good mood today. He doesn't seem at all upset over what happened last night… or other things that have gone on since you guys arrived."

"Oh, no, everything's much better. We made up last night," Mom said with a sly smile on her lips.

Clearing her throat, Fiona was quick to change the subject. "Looks like we may need to breakout the winter coats after all." Looking across the seat, she realized that her mother was sporting her thermal Columbia jacket. *Floridians.* "Oh! I'd better call Nathan and tell him what I figured out last night." She reached for the blue-tooth button on her steering wheel. Nathan's phone rang and rang and rang, until they pulled into the school parking lot. Wrinkling her nose in disappointment, Fiona disconnected. "He's probably in a meeting. I'll call him a little later. Well, here we are. Brace yourself, Mom. Remember, I don't teach ninth grade literature—I teach kindergarten, and it's the day before Christmas break. This could be a lot like Normandy."

Her mom snorted. "I think you're exaggerating, Fiona."

"You'd better hope I am."

The kindergartners were surprisingly quiet and cooperative during the party. Fiona attributed the good behavior to the stranger, her mother, being in the classroom. She also wondered if the children's cooperation was in anticipation of a visit from a special person—Santa. Many of the little girls, including Lizzie and Carly, had asked when he was expected. Fiona's heart sank every time she had to explain she simply wasn't sure if he had time to visit. It was a lie of course—she had no Santa coming at all, but she felt it was a kind lie.

Lincoln Parrish took the opportunity to announce with glee, "He's not comin' cuz he ain't real!"

"He's *not* real," Fiona corrected.

"See? Even Ms. Quinn says he ain't real," Lincoln declared, victoriously.

Fiona rolled her eyes.

While her mom kept the children busy with a craft of making a bird feeder out of a pinecone slathered with peanut butter and then rolled in birdseed, Fiona made another attempt at contacting Nathan. No Luck. He still wasn't answering. Maybe it was a good sign. Maybe he had a hot lead in the case.

By eleven o'clock the party was coming close to an end. The students only had a half-day of school. Fiona sat the children at the tables for cookies and punch. While her mom walked from child to child, making sure they weren't spilling their punch, Fiona dialed Nathan's cell once again. No answer. She hoped that another Santa hadn't been murdered, but decided to call Tavia to see if she knew of his whereabouts.

"No, haven't seen Nathan this morning, sorry. Was your father upset last night?" Tavia asked.

"Why would he be? I'm a grown woman who makes her own decisions. I don't need my dad's approval."

"Your mom smoothed things over, didn't she?"

Fiona sighed. "Something like that."

She no sooner ended her conversation with Tavia when her classroom door burst open. "Ho! Ho! Ho!" a fat jolly man dressed in a cheap Santa suit called out, as he stepped into the room with a sack over his shoulder. Fiona's eyes brightened—her mom's beamed. It was Nathan.

"Santa!" Fiona announced loudly.

"You were expecting the Easter Bunny?" Nathan/Santa inquired, as the children, even Lincoln Parrish, rushed toward him all talking at once. "One at a time! One at a time! If you've been good, I've got a treat for each one of you. Ho! Ho! Ho!"

"Lincoln hasn't been very good. He doesn't believe in you, Santa!" Carly proclaimed, while pointing an accusing finger at the red-faced boy.

A sudden hush fell over the students. Fiona watched while their eyes rotated from Lincoln to Santa and back again. She knew they were wondering what the jolly old elf would do about the skeptic among them. The question had crossed her mind as well.

Taking a seat at the teacher's desk, Nathan/Santa lifted Carly onto his lap. "That doesn't mean he's bad. It just means he needs to come and take a good tug on my beard."

Fiona's eyes widened. Mom cupped a hand over her mouth. It seemed like a risky proposition. Faux beards weren't known to stay on very well—especially when pulled.

Lincoln was up to the task. Puffing out his little chest, he marched past his slack-jawed wide eyed classmates to take a handful of the beard. Biting her lip, Fiona winced. Mom moved her hand from her mouth to her eyes.

Lincoln tugged.

The children moved in closer.

He tugged again, and the children moved a little closer.

Agitated, Lincoln tugged and tugged and tugged to no avail.

The beard stayed in place.

The room erupted with the children's laughter while they clapped their hands merrily.

From her perch on Nathan/Santa's lap, Carly sang out, "See Lincoln, he *is* real!"

Nathan/Santa laughed, "Ho! Ho! Ho! Snickers for everyone— you're all very good girls and boys!" He gave Lincoln and Carly full-size Snickers bars, and then proceeded to hand them out to the rest of the children.

"Wow! *Full-size* Snickers, Santa. How generous." Fiona pointed out.

"Santa should never down-size," Nathan/Santa said, then from deep in his pocket, he pulled out a bite-size bar to hold it out to the strawberry-blonde teacher. With a wink he said, "But not for you, Ms. Quinn. I know you're always watching your figure." He leaned in close to whisper, "As am I."

"*Santa*," Fiona scolded.

Stepping up for her turn, Lizzie Thomas asked, "Where's your elf, Santa?"

"My elf?"

"Yeah, the one who was with you at the mall? The one with the purple hair."

"My elf with the *purple* hair?" he repeated. The little girl nodded. He said, "Um…er…she has the day off today. But I'll be talking with her later this afternoon, and I'll make sure I tell her hello for you. All the elves will be on my sleigh tomorrow night, for sure!"

The children clapped and jumped up and down at the mention of Christmas Eve and Santa's sleigh.

Shushing them, Fiona asked, "Okay, does everyone have a candy bar?" The children responded with a resounding, yes! She added, "Let's all thank Santa for his truly wonderful generous visit, and then get ready for bus calls."

The children clapped. Several little girls, including Lizzie and Carly, gave Nathan/Santa a big hug and a kiss. Lincoln Parrish stood off to the side, studying him intensely. Nathan/Santa offered his hand to the boy, and they shook. Fiona smiled. An understanding had past between them, and with that, Lincoln set off with the rest of his classmates to get ready for home.

Fiona and her mom were relieved when all the children were stuffed in their jackets and safely on their buses for the ride home. The large open-area kindergarten classroom was quiet at last. The adrenaline rush from the busy day was wearing off, and both were starting to feel the effects from their lack of sleep the night before.

They sat at one of the children's work tables, trying to perk up by drinking coffee, while waiting for Nathan to return from changing into his regular clothing.

"Fiona, didn't you say that you've never met Nathan's mother?" Mom asked.

"No, I haven't."

Mom's eyebrows shot upward. "I thought you said you've been dating for ten months. You've never met his mother in all that time?"

Fiona took another sip of her coffee. "That's right."

"Don't you think that's strange? Why wouldn't he introduce you to his mother?" She gasped. "What if she doesn't really exist? What if she was killed when he was a young child? Maybe she was *murdered* and he suffers from some sort of traumatic disorder. Maybe that's what encouraged him to become a homicide detective."

Fiona snorted. "Seriously, Mom? You're being a little melodramatic, don't you think? I mean, does *Evelyn* really exist?"

Her mom raised her palm in a granting fashion. "It's strange— that's all I'm saying."

"Noted."

Nathan stepped into the room. Fiona and her mother were a little taken aback. The Santa costume was gone. He was now sporting his dark slacks, dress shirt, tie, and a light jacket, but he was still wearing the beard. The women exchanged befuddled glances.

Fiona said, "I can't thank you enough for the party, Nathan. You are a lifesaver. Where on earth did you get a Santa costume on such short notice?"

"Turns out Wyatt's dad had one. It wasn't as upscale as the one your uncle wore, but it worked," Nathan explained.

With a giggle in her voice, Fiona asked, "It sure did, thank you again, but…did you forget to take *something* off?"

"Nope. I can't get it off. I glued it on real good, and now it's stuck."

"What kind of glue did you use?"

"Super."

Fiona grimaced. "Oh, Nathan. *Ouch.*"

"Yeah, maybe I didn't think this through as well as I should have. Now I think I'm gonna have to soak it in hot water to loosen it up. I'm a little worried skin is gonna come off with it. I'll do that later when I get home so nobody has to listen to me screaming like a little girl. I'll just have to go about the investigation with it on for now." He scrubbed his fingers through it thoughtfully. "Hm, it may prove to have some benefits."

With a chuckle in her voice, Fiona held up a piece of paper. "You have more than a beard with benefits. I think I've cracked the code, and yes, it was easy-peasy, once I caught on. Look—" Nathan pulled up a tiny chair and sat down—his knees were almost to his chin. Laying the note in front of him, she continued. "I still believe that the SN stands for Saint Nick, and the numbers after the initials represent the mall where the Santa is working. See?" She pointed to her list. "SN-200, I believe that means the Monroeville Mall, because its address is *200* Mall Circle Drive. Watch…SN-570, that's the Beaver Valley Mall. Its address is 570 Beaver Valley Mall Boulevard. It makes sense, look down my list, all the numbers match up to the mall's addresses. Like I said, easy-peasy, yet if you didn't understand the code, it would look like nothing. But I still don't know what the A or E after the numbers represent. A shift? Like, afternoon or evening? I thought each mall only employs one Santa, but maybe not. Wait… now that I think about it, Uncle Wilbur didn't always work at the same time. Sometimes he worked afternoon and sometimes *evening*. There it is! I'm right. Afternoon—evening. Sooo easy, I should've had my students work on it. It would have been a great exercise with simple numbers and letters."

Laughing, Fiona's mom clapped her hands.

Nathan smiled. "I think you're right, Fiona. I hadn't had time to look at the list. And it was a simple code—as you suggested it would be. It's no mystery why I latched on to this one, Mrs. Quinn. Your daughter is beautiful, smart, sweet, and a sleuth to boot."

"She's a keeper, Nathan," Mom put in.

"*Mom—*"

Nathan laughed. "Indeed she is, Mrs. Quinn, indeed she is." Gathering up the list, he stood. "You do realize that this information is inadmissible as evidence in the case, right? The note that you found in the dumpster was obtained illegally. The information may be exactly what I need, but I can never divulge where it came from or that I ever used it."

Sheepishly, Fiona replied, "Sorry about that, Nathan."

"Don't be. We'll find out who did this, and we'll have evidence that we *can* use when we do. That said, let's try to work within the boundaries of the law, okay?" Shamefully, Fiona and her mom nodded. Standing, Nathan said, "Well, I'd love to stay a little longer, but I've got an appointment with a purple-haired elf."

## Ten

When Nathan arrived at Characters for All Occasions on Smallman Street, he was not only disappointed, but surprised as well. Instead of the surly purple-haired Nonatha manning the counter, he found none other than the cordial neon pink-haired, Bunny. She was coming out of a back room behind the counter with a Santa costume draped over her arm, while talking on her cell phone.

"You've got to be patient. Don't worry, it'll be there on time." She jumped when the bell on the door jingled as Nathan let it swung closed behind him. "Gotta go. I've got a customer."

Bunny disconnected the call and tossed the cell onto the counter. She appeared to be just as surprised to see the detective as he was to see her. Smiling brightly she said, "Hey Nate, can't believe I'd bumped into ya two days in a row. Well, I guess technically it's the same day." Hesitating, she cocked her head to one side. "How'd ya grow a beard so fast?"

"You don't want to know," Nathan said.

"Bet I do. Anyway, what can I do for ya?" Bunny asked.

"So what's going on here, Bunny? Are you moonlighting?"

She expelled a nervous giggle. "I work here during the Christmas season for my…er…uncle. It gets really busy, and I can use the extra cash. Been doin' it for…um…years."

"Really? For years? And the *owner's* your uncle?"

"Yeah, my uncle Jimmy…um…you might know him as Jim Chezmadia. He's up in the office, do you need him?"

"No, I came looking for Nonatha. Is today her day off?"

"I dunno." She reached under the counter then flopped a schedule book out. "Let me see—" Thumbing through the pages, she cocked her head to one side, squinted, and licked her lips as if she were having difficulty seeing or reading the pages. "Here she is. She's working with the Santa at the Beaver Valley Mall this evening."

"Mr. Warner?"

"No, Paul doesn't work evenings. He doesn't like to drive Route three-sixty-seven in the dark. He's strictly an afternoon Santa."

"You mean Route three-*seventy*-six, don't you?"

Bunny's nervous giggle returned. "Oh, yeah, that's what I meant—three-seventy-six."

"Do all the Santa's work different shifts?"

She shrugged. "Some do. A lot of the boys are pretty old, so they only work the afternoon sittings. Our younger guys will work either—sometimes both in one day. More money, I guess. Mr. Stacy was our oldest Santa, and he worked either shift. Whatta great old guy—God rest his soul."

Nathan eyed the schedule book. "Could you do me a favor?"

She glanced up the staircase and then shrugged. "Sure. I mean, it depends on what ya need."

"Could you make a quick list of who was working what shift on Monday, December twenty-first?"

Picking up a notepad lying next to the phone, Bunny suddenly hesitated. "Well...I should okay that through Jimmy...I mean, *Uncle* Jimmy. Just a minute—"

"No, never mind—"

She was already across the room and starting up the stairs. "No really, it's okay, he's really a sweetie—he'll do pretty much anything I ask."

"I don't think so," Nathan muttered under his breath.

When Bunny reached the top of the stairs, she draped the costume that still dangled over her arm on the railing, then she knocked on the door.

A scowling Jim opened the door and yanked a cigar from his lips. "What do you want, Bernadette?"

"This detective would like a list of the Santa's—"

Pushing her aside, Jim peered over the railing. "Look McGarrett—"

"Landry, Detective Nathan Landry," Nathan said.

"Whatever! I told you, I don't give out employee information without a warrant. Do I need to call your supervisor and file a complaint?"

"No, sir, I just wanted to talk with Nonatha, but I see she's not here."

"No, she's not. So unless you want me to file harassment charges, you'd best be on your way. Bernadette—get back to work."

Red faced, Bunny scurried down the staircase.

Embarrassed for Bunny, but needing to move on, Nathan headed for the door.

"Nate! Wait," Bunny called. She went to the counter, wrote on the notepad, and gave it to him. "If ya ever need me, for *anything*, here's my number."

Apprehensively, Nathan took the paper from her fingers. "Yeah… thanks, Bunny. See ya."

"I hope so."

Feeling the flush on his cheeks, he hurried out the door. Before crinkling the note to stuff it into his pocket, he glanced down at it. He stopped. The cell number she'd scribbled down was, 244-555-2345. Only the fives and the threes were written backward. It appeared to Nathan that Bunny was dyslexic—a disorder where people see things backward or reverse words and numbers, and she had probably gone undiagnosed as a child. The condition may have aided in her life as it was at present.

He folded the note and shoved it in his pocket. The paper looked to be the same as the paper from the note Fiona had retrieved from the dumpster. Problem was he couldn't turn it into forensics to find out because Fiona's note had been attained in an illegal manner. He'd have to find another way.

—w—

It was barely a mile drive home from school to Oxford Street, and still Fiona had to fight the urge to lay her head on the steering wheel for a nap. She had every intention of changing into a pair of comfy sweats, turning off her cell phone, and taking a two-hour nap when she got home. She was even considering closing her bedroom door so Harriett couldn't get in. She'd have the entire bed to herself for a change. They passed the garbage truck, as they turned off Warriors Road onto Oxford Street.

"Hope Dad remembered to put the trash out," Fiona said.

There was no response from her mother. She glanced across the seat to find her mother snoozing with her head tilted back against the headrest. Arriving home, Fiona parked the Mini Cooper in front of the walk, taking note of the emptied trash can lying on its side.

She nudged her mother to wake. "C'mon, Mom, you should rest somewhere a bit more comfortable."

Dragging the trashcan up the walk, she deposited it next to the porch until she had the strength to schlep it around back. Fiona and her mom made their way into the house to be greeted by five zealous Yorkies and one Maltese, dancing and jumping and yipping for joy around their ankles.

"Hello, my babies, oh, and you too, Harriet," Mom cooed. "C'mon, Mommy's gonna take a nappy-poo." She started for the stairs.

Fiona scooped Harriet up, then poked her head in the living room to find her father reading the paper. "Thanks for putting the trash out for me, Dad."

He peeked over the paper. "No problem, sweetie. I couldn't get that old star to light no matter what I did, so I got rid of it. I would've went to the store and got you a new one if I had a car."

Fiona's eyes snapped to the top of the tree—it was naked. Suddenly she was wide awake and filled with urgency. "You threw grandma's star out!" Without waiting for his response, she dropped Harriet into his arms and raced out the door to jump into the car. She spun the Mini Cooper in a circle in the middle of Oxford to speed down the street toward Warriors Road.

—m—

Nancy closed the door behind Fiona. "Garrett, how could you?"

"I…I thought I was doing her a favor. It was old and broken, Nancy. I tried to fix it, but it just didn't work. I *told* her that it might not be fixable. I didn't think she'd be *this* upset. Where's she going?"

"After the garbage truck would be my guess. I can't believe you did this. You know how sentimental Fiona is. How could you throw the star away without discussing it with her?"

"You're right. You're absolutely right. I'm sorry. Sometimes we parents do stupid thoughtless things."

"*We* parents? How did I get involved? I was nowhere near the scene of the crime," Nancy stated.

"You were last night." He let out a regretful sighed. "I've got to make it up to her somehow. Call Chad. Tell him to meet us at the Greentree Inn for dinner at seven. It isn't much, but it's something." Pressing his hands helplessly into his pockets, he looked out the window, letting out another careworn sigh. "I feel like such a jerk. I sure hope she can get that star back."

— ⋙ —

The garbage truck's engine droned like a sickly troll as it slowly eased up the steep hill on Warriors Road. Fiona honked her horn repeatedly as she drove up to the rear of the truck. The man hanging on the back looked at her with furrowed brows and a scowl. She honked again, and the truck came to a juddering, squeaky halt.

Without looking in her direction, the man jumped down from his perch on the truck to pick up a trashcan at the end of the next walk. Fiona slid from the car to jog toward him.

"Excuse me," she said, breathlessly. "I need my trash back. I'm the 529 Oxford Street pickup."

"Yeah, right, lady, all the garbage is marked with the street numbers. Whatta ya think this is, a *filing system*?" the man said, curtly.

"If you haven't run the compactor yet, my trash bags should be easy to find—they're the pink scented bags, and there should only be two," Fiona explained, in a panicked tone.

The man stopped mid-chore to take in her pleading expression. Dropping the can he'd just picked up, he waved a yielding hand. "Okay, you're just lucky. We usually run the compactor every five stops, but some of your neighbors must be away for the holidays so we didn't get as much trash. I'll look." He called to the driver, "Hey, Roy! Hold up a minute. I gotta look in the back for some bags."

After her close encounter with trash the night before, Fiona didn't care to get too close to the truck, but she eased her way a little nearer to take a look along with the man. "There they are!" she called out, pointing inside the hull. He pulled two pink bags from the truck's slipper, and dropped them on the ground before her. "I see it! It's in this one." She pulled the star from the bag. "Thank you so much. I'm so sorry I interrupted your schedule."

"Eh, you're not the first hysterical woman to chase us down. I'm glad you got your star back. Merry Christmas, lady." After tossing Fiona's bags and the contents of the can at the current stop into the slipper, he climbed back onto the truck and waved the driver forward.

Fiona leaned a hip against her car, hugging the star to her chest. She whispered, "Not yet. Not. Just. Yet."

Before he made the drive all the way up Route three-seventy-six to the Beaver Valley Mall to talk with Nonatha, Nathan decided it was time to stop by Three Brothers Dry Cleaning in Robinson Township. He parked his SUV next to a white van in the lot. As he stepped into the business, Fiona swept into his mind. He had to chuckle to himself at the thought of the tiny blonde climbing around in the dry cleaner's dumpster the night before—whatta sight that would've been!

A tall slender dark-haired man who was staring warily at Nathan's beard met him at the counter. Clearing his throat, he inquired, "Can I help you?"

Nathan opened his jacket to flash his badge. "Detective Nathan Landry, Pittsburgh Homicide. I was hoping you can answer a few questions for me—" Squinting, he leaned over the counter to read the man's nametag. "Keith."

"I'll do my best, Detective."

"Is this the dry cleaner's where Characters for All Occasions sends their Santa costumes?"

Keith's lips curled into a smirk. "Are you missing your costume, Detective?"

Smiling back at the clever remark, Nathan stroked the fake beard stuck to his face. "No, I keep mine safely tucked in the trunk of my car at all times. But I like to wear the beard." Pumping his eyebrows, he leaned over the counter to whisper, "The ladies are really into it. All. Year. Long."

His sarcasm squelched, Keith pulled back. "I see. Well… Detective…to answer your question, yes, we do clean the Santa costumes for Jim Chezmadia. Is there a problem?"

Nathan curled several strands of the beard around his forefinger, thoughtfully. "Well, yes, there kinda is a small problem. As you may have heard one of their Santas was murdered."

"Yes, Wilbur Stacy—God rest his soul."

"Yeah, that's how everyone seems to feel. Anyway, his suit was the only thing to be stolen during a robbery. Mr. Stacy was just unfortunate enough to be killed. That said, you may also know that another Santa under Mr. Chezmadia's employ had his costume stolen, so we have to wonder, what is the connection between the stolen costumes?"

"I assure you that I don't have the foggiest idea—I just clean the costumes, Detective. About a week or so ago, Jim requested that the costumes be cleaned, so we picked them up and we cleaned them—that's pretty much how our business works."

"The request came *directly* from Jim Chezmadia?"

"Well, I don't exactly know who called. It could have been one of the girls—it prob'ly was. Jim doesn't usually bother himself with such trivial tasks."

"I see. One of the Santas told me that they're cleaned often," Nathan said.

"Um...some are, I guess. Not all of them. I really don't know why."

"You picked the costumes up in the van parked outside?" Nathan asked. He reached into his pocket and pulled out a small piece of candy.

"Yes, that's our brand new pickup and delivery van. We haven't even had time to have our business logo painted on it. Perhaps after the holiday rush," Keith said.

Nathan fumbled with the foiled candy, and then pop it into his mouth. He could see Keith watching him with impatient eyes.

Nathan turned to look out the large window at the van.

"It's a very nice van. Very clean looking. I guess that's a good thing for a dry cleaner," Nathan said, around a mouthful of chocolate.

"Yes, I suppose it is."

He pulled another foil square out from his pocket. "Snickers?"

"No. No, thank you."

"How long were the costumes in your possession, and how many costumes did they turn in?" Nathan inquired, while eyeing a notepad on the counter—it too looked like the same paper from the note Fiona had retrieved from the dumpster.

"Um, well, I believe the costumes were only here for about twenty-four hours. We can't keep them for very long during the holidays, that's for sure." Keith reached under the counter to produce a small notebook. After flipping through the pages, he said, "Says here that six costumes were turned in, and six costumes were delivered back to Jim's shop on the twentieth of the month."

"In that van?"

"Yes, I believe we've established that it is our pickup and delivery van."

"Yes, we did. Thanks, Keith." Nathan turned to leave. Scratching deep in the beard, he turned back. "Don't you think that's strange? That the character shop would have the costumes cleaned so late in the season? I mean, if it were me, I'd have the costumes cleaned before the season began, rather than a few days before Christmas. Of course, I don't know much about the character costume business or the dry cleaning businesses. I'm just sayin', it seems backwards."

"Well, maybe some of the Santa's complained that they weren't clean, or maybe something happened to some of the costumes," Keith suggested.

"That's true. Ya know, ya gotta give those guys a lot of credit. Little kids can do a lot of things to soil a costume—they've got sticky fingers, they spill stuff. I bet some of them even wipe their little noses on good ol' Saint Nick."

"Well, yes…children can be messy, that's for sure—"

"One has to have a lot of patience when it comes to working with children. As you can see, I played Santa earlier today. Those kids are all over ya. Do you have children, Keith?"

"No. Do you, Detective?"

"No, I don't. Someday, maybe. Six costumes came in from the character shop, you said?" He patted his chest and the pockets of his slacks.

"That's what I said, *six*," Keith replied.

"I can't find my notebook. I'll bet that I'll forget that number. Could I borrow a piece of paper from your notepad there?"

By his fingertips, Keith slid the pad across the counter toward him.

Still digging at the beard, Nathan ripped a piece of paper from the pad, jotted down the number six on it, and then winced. "Man, these beards sure do get itchy after a while. Like I said, gotta give those department store Saint Nick's a lotta credit—there's way more suffering to the job than one would think." Nathan waved and made his exit.

—⋙—

Keith sighed in relief as he watched the detective depart.

As the shop door eased closed, a man slipped into the room from a door located behind the counter. "Who was that?"

"He was one of Pittsburgh's finest. To tell you the truth, I don't think he could catch a criminal to save his soul." Shaking his head, Keith snorted. "Whatta hot mess, Bobby. He was a real hot mess."

## Eleven

"Hey, Mr. Warner, how are you today?" Nathan asked, finding Paul Warner standing outside Macy's Department Store. The old guy was smoking a cigarette while hooked to a mobile oxygen machine on wheels. Paul had a garment bag slung over his shoulder but wore his Santa boots tugged up over his blue jeans.

Paul Warner's eyes narrowed, studying the man approaching him. "Detective Landry?"

"Yeah, I don't usually wear a white beard. I was playing Santa this morning for a kindergarten class, and well, it's kinda stuck."

"Pilgrim," Paul laughed, initiating a bout of coughing. "Excuse… me, my…emphysema's actin'…up."

"Yeah, I see you're all attached to that oxygen tank."

"I hook up mostly when I smoke," Paul said, around the coughs.

"Wow." Pointing at the garment bag, Nathan said, "Looks like they replaced your Santa costume."

"Yeah, guess they had no choice. They need an afternoon Santa here at Beaver Valley. Sam's got a day job. He can only work evenings. Sooo…yinz didn't find no prints at my house then?"

"No, sorry to say we didn't find anything to help our investigation, but we're pluggin' along," Nathan said, as he pulled open the door to enter the mall.

Paul tossed the cigarette to the cement, crushing it under his heel. "Well, good luck with that."

—⚬—

The line to Santa Claus stretched all the way to the fountain in the middle of the Beaver Valley Mall. Last minute gift requests or perhaps overtly busy parents were trying to make sure the children visited and got their photo taken with the main man of the season. Nathan was on the receiving end of many a stare from the kids and adults alike, as he strode to the front of the line sporting his white beard. Clad as a not so jolly elf, Nonatha spotted him immediately as he drew near. Her churlish expression turned more unpleasant the closer he got.

She shoved a small candy cane at a little boy, lifted him off the Santa's lap, and called, "Next!" She pushed the boy toward his grinning mother, and then she flopped the next little girl from the line onto Santa's lap before she turned to Nathan. "What're you doing here? And what's that thing on your face? Looks like you're wearing someone's dead cat."

"It's nice to see you too, *Elf* Nonatha. I came to ask you a few questions," Nathan said.

"*Seriously*? Can't you see I'm kinda busy?" Brushing past him, she grabbed a camera off a nearby folding table to focus in on the now crying girl perched on Santa's lap.

"'Tis the season, I suppose. Ya know, I was thinking, well, I was more *remembering* than thinking. Anyway, the day I stopped by your shop there was a white van parked outside. Did it belong to Three Brothers Dry Cleaning?"

The little girl on Santa's lap was now in full-blown shrieking mode. The Santa was holding her up for her mother to claim.

Pitching the camera on the table, Nonatha blew out an irritated breath. "I have no idea. I don't keep tabs on what vehicles the dry cleaner uses. Can you go now? *Next!*"

"The guy who delivers the cleaned costumes—"

"Bob Schlemmer," Nonatha said over her shoulder, as she grabbed the hands of a set of twins to lead them toward an apprehensive Santa, while the twins stared, wide eyed, at Nathan.

"Did you give him a note that day?"

"What? I dunno! What makes you think I gave him a note?" She hoisted the children onto Santa's lap. The twin's mother rushed forward to fluff the little girl twin's dress. Nonatha rolled her eyes as she snatched the camera from the table.

"He dropped it as he was going out the door. I picked it up for him," Nathan explained.

"Okay, yeah sure, why not? I prob'ly gave Bob a note, what about it? Hey, kids! Smile for the camera!"

"Do you remember what was on the note? Do you pass notes to that driver very often?" Nathan pressed.

"Look *Rumpelstiltskin*, I'm really busy here. Yeah, sometimes I give the driver's notes. Sometimes I give them checks—prob'ly payment for their services. That's how business's work. They provide a service, and we pay them. Now go scare the little children someplace else, would'ja?"

Nathan glanced at the line of children waiting to visit with Santa. Many of the kids were staring at him wide-eyed and slack-jawed. Some were clinging to their parent's legs, while others were crying, hiding their faces. A majority of the moms were trying to soothe their little ones, while the fathers were glaring at him.

Nonatha was right about one thing—it was time to leave.

—⋙—

**Wednesday evening, Greentree Inn,**
"Tomorrow is Christmas Eve and we're no closer to knowing who killed Uncle Wilbur than we were yesterday," Fiona complained after ordering the chicken picatta.

Chad said, "These things take time, Fiona. This isn't a CSI program on TV. This is reality—a real murder. It won't be solved in a one-hour segment. It may take weeks, possibly months."

"I know, and I hate myself for being so impatient. I just don't want Uncle Wilbur to be laid to rest with people thinking that he was somehow involved with drugs."

"I really don't believe anyone thinks that, sweetheart," Fiona's dad said, while returning his menu to the waitress.

"I'm not so sure, Garrett. I got a call from Aunt Ruthie yesterday, and she was asking questions along those lines," Mom put in.

Dropping her elbow to the table and her chin into her palm, Fiona sighed.

Fiona's mom patted her on the shoulder. "Look, Fiona, we all know it's not true. Uncle Wilbur would never get involved in anything that's against the law. We know it, and everyone in the family knows it. Even if Aunt Ruthie is worrying about it. Hey! I've got just the thing to cheer us up. Let's go to the mall and do some Christmas shopping. Macy's will be open until midnight, and oh, the bargains. What do you say, Fiona? It'll be just like old times."

"No, sounds like it'll be better than old times. Back in the day, you'd drag me from my nice warm bed at four a.m. on Black Friday. We wouldn't get home until seven that night. It was beyond exhausting. But yeah, I'm behind in my shopping so let's do it."

Mom clapped her hands. "Oh, goody!"

"Hey, how's everybody in the Quinn clan doing tonight?" Nathan said, as he plopped a kiss on Fiona's cheek and pulled up a chair. He turned to the waitress. "I'll have the lasagna. Italian dressing on the side of my salad, please. Oh, and garlic knots—double order. Thanks."

"Nathan? I didn't expect you tonight. How did you know we were here?" Fiona asked.

"I texted him, dear," her mother said.

"You text Nathan? How did you get his number?"

"We exchanged numbers the other night. Didn't we, Nan?" Nathan said.

Smiling brightly, Fiona's mom nodded.

"*Nan?*" Fiona repeated, shell-shocked.

Leaning in close to his sister, Chad whispered into her ear. "Nice beard. Is this some kind of weird kinky Santa thing you two got going for the holidays?"

"Shut up, Chad," Fiona hissed out the side of her mouth.

Chad let go of a wicked chortle.

"I just discovered that one of the owners of Three Brothers Dry Cleaning lives three doors down from you, Fiona. Why didn't you tell me? What do you know about the Schlemmer's?" Nathan asked.

"Well, I really don't know—"

"Mom used to be engaged to Keith Schlemmer. Fiona said he dropped by the house the other night," Chad said, and then realizing that the table had fallen completely silent, he looked up to take in his dinner companions' faces.

Fiona glowered at him.

Their mother looked like she'd just swallowed a rabid squirrel.

Their father's face was suddenly flushed with irritation, and Nathan was staring at Fiona with one eyebrow arched as if she'd just belched without saying excuse me.

"In all the excitement, I think there was something we forgot to tell you, Nathan."

"*Really*? And when were you planning to tell me that one of the suspects in your uncle's murder case had dropped by for a little meet and greet?"

"Keith Schlemmer is a suspect in the case?" her mother exclaimed a little too loudly.

"Of course he is, *Nan*. We found the note in *his* dumpster, didn't we?" Fiona more scolded than asked.

"What note? What are you talking about?" her father asked.

Fiona was in a panic to explain. "It wasn't so much a meet and greet as it was a lost and found. Dad lost Keith—Mom's dog, and Keith—Keith Schlemmer, found him, and brought Keith—Mom's dog, home. That's when Keith—Keith Schlemmer, realized that the woman he was returning Keith—"

"Your mom's dog?"

"Yes, Mom's dog, Keith. That's when he realized that Mom was his former lover—" Fiona winced. "I mean, fiancé—Keith Schlemmer, not the dog. Nothing really went on, other than Dad got hot under the collar because Keith—Mom's former fiancé, was in the foyer, and Mom was acting all—anyway, this all happened *before* Uncle Wilbur was murdered and we went dumpster diving." Raking her fingers through her hair, she took in a deep breath. "I'm not hungry anymore."

"What note?" her father asked again.

"Okay, time for some damage control. Tell me what you know about the Schlemmers'. There must be three brothers, but I can only locate two, Keith and Bob. Is there actually three, or is that just the name of the business for some really strange reason?" Nathan asked.

Everyone turned to look at Fiona's mom. She said, "Yes, there are three of them, but I can't for the life of me remember all their names. Of course there's Keith—"

"*Of course*," Fiona's dad snarled.

"And I remember Bobby Schlemmer. He was younger than Keith. But I'm having trouble coming up with the third name. The oldest brother was five or six years older than we were, so we didn't have a lot of contact with him. And...and his last name wasn't Schlemmer, as I recall. Wait a minute...he was from Keith's mother's first marriage." Mom sat back against her seat, trying to remember. By the frustration in her expression, everyone could see that the name simply wasn't coming back to her.

"It's okay," Nathan said in a calm soothing voice. "Let's have a nice dinner. Maybe the less you think about it, the name will pop into your mind."

"I agree. It's like when I've lost something. If I stop looking for it, it usually turns up," Fiona said.

"Like Nathan's face?" Chad whispered to Fiona, who shot him a warning look.

The group fell silent once again, and the waitress arrived with an assistant. They were toting two large trays. She and the assistant set the drink orders, salads, and two large baskets of bread on the table.

"Your dinners will be out soon," the waitress promised, then she and her assistant returned to the kitchen.

As if to give Mom all the room she needed to remember Keith Schlemmer's stepbrother's name, everyone dug into their salads without talking.

"What note?" Fiona's dad asked again.

## Twelve

The mall was jam-packed with last minute shoppers in search of last minute bargains. Fiona and her mom weaved their way through the throng toward the entrance of Macy's Department Store. "I just can't believe that I can't remember Keith's brother's name. It's just not coming to me, Fiona. It's so frustrating. You don't think I'm getting dementia, do you?" Mom said.

"No, Mom, you're not getting dementia. You're as sharp as a tack. Relax. Don't think about it. It'll come to you." Stopping at the counter in the jewelry department, Fiona eyed the men's watches. "Does Chad have a watch?"

"I don't know," Mom replied, while lifting a sparkling rhinestone necklace from the display rack. "He takes that silly cell phone with him everywhere. I swear it's attached to him just like a kidney. I think he uses it as a watch. Lord knows he uses it for everything else. I read somewhere that the sales in watches are way down because of cell phones. Too bad. Watches are so elegant—I think so anyway."

"Well, that settles that. Chad isn't elegant or *eloquent* on any level. Looks like it's a hoodie for him again this year. Maybe a Pirates hoodie. I got him a Steelers last year, or was it Penguins?" Fiona turned to head for the men's department.

"Wait. I'm going to buy this necklace. It'll go perfectly with dress I plan to wear to the Christmas Eve wine tasting that the McCune's are putting on." Her mother stepped into the line at the jewelry counter beside a woman with neon pink hair, wearing jeans that were way too tight and a bright green T-shirt that had the sentence, Jingle my Bells, scrolled in sequins across the chest. Fiona immediately recognized the woman—Bunny from jail.

Gasping, Fiona grabbed her mother's arm to pull her backward, letting three women ahead of her in the line. The women kept a distance from Bunny, while whispering to each other.

"Fiona...what are you doing?" Her mother growled.

"Shhh...see that woman?"

"What woman? What's the matter with you?"

"The woman with the pink hair getting ready to pay for her stuff. That's the woman we were in jail with. What's her name? Bunny, I think." Her mother's head snapped toward the cashier. "Don't look! Okay...look now, but try to be discreet."

Furtively, her mother peeked around the two women she'd just let into the line ahead of her. "You're right. That's her," she whispered over her shoulder to Fiona.

"What's she buying?" Fiona asked.

"I don't know. I can't see."

"I'm sorry, this isn't the correct amount, ma'am," she heard the salesgirl say to Bunny. "The price is seventy-one dollars, not seventeen."

"I thought it was on sale," Bunny said.

"It is, ma'am, for seventy-one dollars. Do you still want it?"

Bunny crinkled her nose, and then shrugged. "Ugh! I do that all the time—switch the numbers all around. It's really aggravating. Oh, well, I've got the cash. Why not? Tis the season, right?" she asked the ladies in the line behind her. Taking a half step back, they politely chuckled and nodded their agreement. Smiling, Bunny dug through her purse for the extra money.

"Bet I know where she got the cash," Fiona's mom said under her breath.

"I feel bad for her. She must suffer from dyslexia. I've got a little girl in my class who inverts numbers and letters all the time. It's so hard to stay on track with learning her numbers and to read. She goes to special support classes. Maybe Bunny never did. Dyslexia goes undiagnosed a lot," Fiona said, while she watched Bunny gather her bag and hurry from the store.

—⁓—

Fiona was awakened with a start. Someone was shaking her feverishly. "Fiona…Fiona—" the woman whispered. She jerked to her elbows to find her mother standing over her—almost nose to nose.

"Mom…what is it? Is the house on fire?" Blinking, while brushing her hair from her face, she tried to focus.

"No…I've remembered."

Suddenly, something was bouncing on the bed. Harriet growled from beneath the blankets. Fiona shuffled around to find Keith padding over top of the Maltese. Keith, the dog—not Keith Schlemmer. Thank God.

Trying to force herself to full consciousness, Fiona asked, "You've remembered what?"

"The name, Keith Schlemmer's brother's name from his mother's first marriage," her mom explained.

"You mean Keith Schlemmer's stepbrother's name?"

"Yes. It was Jimmy."

Fiona sat straight up. "Jimmy what?"

"I'm not absolutely sure, Ch…Ch…Chesney, I think."

"You mean like the country singer?" Fiona asked around a yawn.

"What country singer?"

"I dunno. His name's Lenny or Denny or something like that, but his last name is definitely Chesney."

"Maybe, I don't think so." She sat down on the bed. Keith crawled into her lap. "No, no, that's not it. Ch…Ch—" Her face brightened with recollection. "Chezmadia! That's it. I'm certain. His name was Jimmy *Chezmadia*. You've got to call Nate."

"*Nate*? Since when do you call Nathan, Nate?"

"Don't you call him Nate?"

"I do not."

"Well, whatever you call the young man, call him now, and tell him that I've remembered Jimmy Chezmadia's name. And then get dressed, we're taking a ride," Mom said, as she tucked the Yorkie under her arm and started toward the bedroom door.

"It's two o'clock in the morning. *Nate's* probably sleeping. I'll send him a text, just in case we can't get ahold of him in the morning—like the last time." She grabbed her cell from the nightstand and thumbed a text message. When she looked up, she realized that her mother was dressed in black. "Why are you dressed like a cat burglar, and where do you want to go at two in the morning?"

"We're going to stakeout Three Brothers Dry Cleaning. If Keith Schlemmer's involved in a cocaine ring, we're going to find out. Everybody knows that drug people work in the wee hours of the morning," her mom said.

"Drug people? What? Wait. This *is not* our job. This is *Nathan's* job. I can't go breaking the law again. Nathan will kill me."

"Now who's being melodramatic? He's a homicide detective, Fiona. He's not allowed to kill you. Oh, and just a little suggestion, I think you should start calling him Nate. It's so much cuter." Fiona's mouth dropped open. Unaffected, her mom snuggled Keith, the dog, close to her face. "It's like you said, we don't want poor Uncle Wilbur to go to his reward with this ridiculous cocaine business hanging over his head. Aunt Ruthie was more upset than I let on at dinner."

"I'm not going with you, and that's that," Fiona declared, crossing her arms over her chest.

"Suit yourself. I've got your car keys in my pocket, so I'm going with you or without you. Now quit being such a stick in the mud, Fiona Nicole. Get dressed, and get that jar of black face paint." Her mom marched out of the room and down the stairs.

Fiona fell back onto her pillow. "This has to be a terrible dream, or I'm suffering from some kind of cruel deja vu."

From out of the darkness a loud whistle stirred Nathan Landry from his sleep. He rolled over, peeking through weary eyes at the lighted screen of his cell phone lying on his nightstand. Trying to wake and move his stiff fingers, he reached for it to see a text from, Fiona. He pressed the envelope icon, while rubbing his eyes, wondering what his girlfriend could possibly be contacting him about in the middle of the night.

*Mom remembered Keith Schlemmer's stepbrother's name:*
*Jim Chezmadia*
*I hope that's helpful*

The corners of Nathan's lips lifted into a curl. "It's very helpful, darlin'. Very helpful, indeed," he whispered. He dialed the phone, and waited, hoping Tavia would answer.

"Allegheny County Police, Officer Andrews," Tavia said.

"Hey, bestie, can ya do a little research for me since you're working the desk?"

"Who is this?" Tavia asked, wryly.

Nathan snorted. "I'll take that as a solid yes. I need to know where Characters for All Occasions get their costumes. Who's the manufacturer? In country or out?"

"I'm on it," Tavia said.

Disconnecting the call, he was confident she'd have the information he needed within a few hours at the most. He'd be waiting at the door of the costume shop for Mr. Chezmadia bright and early.

She couldn't believe it. Fiona simply could not believe that she was once again driving along the Steubenville Pike at two-thirty in the morning with her mother to return to the scene of their original crime—Three Brothers Dry Cleaning, in Robinson Township. She also couldn't believe her mother insisted on bringing Keith, the dog—*again*.

"Nothing has changed. I can't put him in his kennel or he'll start barking and wake your father and the other dogs," her mom said, in self-defense.

"Mm, I think he's your favorite," Fiona said, while trying to suppress a yawn.

"Got me. But it's not because of Keith Schlemmer, my little Keith is special. We have a special bond."

"You mean he's spoiled."

"Got me again. There's the dry cleaners on the right, just after the traffic light."

"Yes, Mother, I know. I believe I've been here before. Only this time the coast is clear. There's no old man sitting in a car at the intersection to tattle on us."

"Said the kindergarten teacher," Mom teased.

"Mock me if you like, but if we get caught, I'm telling *Nate* that I drove you here under duress."

She eased the Mini Cooper into the parking lot that accommodated four businesses: The Hair-port; State Insurance Agency; Sweet Stuff Bakery, and Three Brothers Dry Cleaning. Because of the ridiculously early hour, the lot was empty, except for a white van parked outside the door of the dry cleaners.

"Park at the far end of the lot. In the corner—near the hair salon. Pull in under that big tree. It's dark there," Mom told her.

*Far end of the lot. In the corner. Under the big tree.* Her mother's directives were getting under Fiona's skin—way under. Maybe it was the lack of a good night's sleep. Maybe it was all the chaos surrounding her perfectly planned holiday. One thing was for sure: next Christmas she was going to the Bahamas!

Blowing out an irritated breath loud enough for her mother to hear, Fiona did as she was instructed. She figured she was lucky that she was able to talk her mother out of wearing the face paint. She also figured that it wouldn't take very long for Mom to get bored, and they could go home, and she could go back to her warm cozy bed—while she still had employment and a boyfriend.

After scanning the parking lot to make sure there weren't any no trespassing signs, Fiona turned the headlights out, adjusted her seat into a comfortable tilt, and closed her eyes. This was her mother's party. Mom could very well watch for the "drug people" on her own, while she tried to catch a few Z's.

"Fiona…Fiona…Fiona—" the voice seemed far away, until the verbal transformed into the physical—shaking her shoulder roughly.

Fiona jumped from the reclined position to a quick panicked horizontal position. "What? What? Are the drug people here?"

"No," Mom said. "I'm hot. I'm having one of my flashes. I haven't had one since I got here, but here it is now. I need you to turn on the car so I can put my window down a bit—quickly, before I combust."

"I would've thought you'd be past all that by now," Fiona groused low and hoarse from sleep.

"Don't I wish?"

Rubbing her eyes, Fiona noticed the windshield and the windows were fogged. Her mother was wiping her sweaty face with the sleeve of her jacket. She also noticed the time, three-thirty a.m. They'd been sitting in the lot for an hour. She was impressed by her mother's staying power. Who knew?

Fiona started the car and pressed the button for the passenger window to lower, and then she turned on the defroster to clear the windshield. If the drug people showed up, and that was a very big *if*, they'd never be able to see them through the steam. Sooner or later, her mother had to realize just how pointless the stakeout was. Fiona was hoping the epiphany would strike her mother very soon.

Fiona's mom stuck her head out the window for air, as did Keith. Fiona settled back into her seat to resume her nap when Keith started to growl low and terse. Fiona opened her right eye just enough to peek at what he was complaining about. His tiny tail was wagging madly. His ears were sucked flat against his little head. His snarl grew louder and fiercer. Well, as fierce as a six pound dog can manage.

"What's wrong with you, Keith?" Mom asked, while brushing her fingers over his ears.

"Maybe he has to go potty," Fiona suggested.

"I wouldn't think—" Before she could finish her sentence, Keith leapt out the window to dash across the parking lot after a mangy yellow alley cat creeping along the sidewalk in front of the insurance agency next to the dry cleaner. "Oh my God! Keith!" Mom shrieked, as she fumbled with the door handle, trying desperately to get out of the car.

Once again, Fiona went from relaxed and reclined to horizontal and horrified in a nanosecond. Finally managing to open the door, her mother jumped from the car to run across the lot after the Yorkie. Just then Fiona saw the headlights from a car coming from the traffic light toward the lot. She wasn't sure if the drug people were arriving, but she didn't want to get caught doing something she should not be doing—not again.

Her mother must've seen the car too. She caught up with Keith, scooped him up, and ducked behind the driver side of the van, as the car pulled into a parking space on the passenger side of the van.

Fiona held her breath, while she squeezed her fingers tightly around the steering wheel until the knuckles turned white. She watched helplessly as two men got out of the car, and walked toward the door of the dry cleaner. One man dug at the door to unlock it. From the distance and the darkness, she didn't recognize either of the men, but one was dragging something behind him. At her angle, she couldn't make out what it was. A tiny red flame lit up through the shadows. He was smoking a cigarette or a cigar or possibly an electronic cigarette. Before entering the shop, he tossed it to the sidewalk to crush it with his foot—which eliminated the E-cigarette.

She clenched her lower lip between her teeth. They were going to get caught—she just knew it. And if the two men who went into the dry cleaners were actually drug runners, she may not have to worry about her employment or her boyfriend. If the men realized that she and her mother were not only in their parking lot at three a.m., but they were spying on them, she and her mother may end up at the bottom of the Allegheny River wearing a pair of cement boots!

Fiona's mom didn't move a muscle as she hunkered down behind the van, holding Keith's snout in her hands so he couldn't bark. Fiona waited, but no lights came on inside the dry cleaners. What could they be doing inside the building without lights?

Hey, wait a minute.

Maybe she was jumping to ridiculous conclusions. Maybe, just maybe, dry cleaners come in very early in the morning to get clothes ready for their business customers. Maybe this was commonplace—especially during the holidays.

Tapping nervous fingers on the steering wheel, Fiona continued to watch the door and the clock. There had been no movement in seven minutes, so she took the chance and flashed her parking lights at her mother as a signal to come back to the car.

It was time to leave—whether her mother liked it or not.

Her mom must've got the idea. Staying low, she trotted across the lot toward the Mini Cooper, while glancing furtively over her shoulder at the dry cleaner and the van. She was only fifteen feet into the move when the door of the dry cleaners opened!

Fiona gasped.

Her mom froze.

She wasn't close enough to make it to the car unnoticed, but she was close to an ornamental tree standing in a landscaped island located in the middle of the lot. She ducked behind the skeletal winter remains of a Japanese maple. Keith struggled in her arms, but Mom held on for dear life.

Fiona dropped her forehead onto the steering wheel—she couldn't bear to watch. She was having visions of Tavia showing up once again to haul them back to jail, or worse, Tavia not being summoned and the thugs fitting them for those cement boots.

Slowly, Fiona dragged her face upward to dare a look. With armfuls of what she assumed to be laundry, wrapped in plastic, the men made their way to the back of the van and pulled open the double doors. Carefully, they placed the clothing onto the floor of the van, then leaving the doors standing open, they went back inside the building.

From her feeble hiding place, Fiona saw her mother let out a relieved breath. Luckily, the men hadn't noticed her. Mom glanced back to the car. Fiona lowered the driver's window, and waved to her mother to make a mad dash. Her mom nodded her understanding. As she pushed to her feet, the rabble-rousing alley cat slunk around the corner of the building to make another appearance. Keith squirmed wrangled and wiggled violently until he was free from her mom's grip. He pounced to the pavement. Mom let out a squeal, as she dashed after her little dog, running directly toward the van!

"No! No! No!" Fiona squeaked, tightening her grip on the steering wheel all the more, as the door to the dry cleaner opened again. The two men were coming back out with another load of laundry in their arms. She couldn't imagine what direction her mother would decide upon, but the good news was the piles of laundry, or whatever they were carrying, was so large that they couldn't see over top of their haul. She could make it back to the car without being detected if she'd make her move *now*.

No…not the decision that her mom—the alleged wild child of the seventies, made.

The cat took refuge under the van, and just as Keith was going in after it, her mom managed to scoop the little dog up and dove into the back of the van!

What?

No!

Fiona was now so horizontal that her head practically went through the roof of the Mini Cooper.

She couldn't believe it! What was her mother thinking?

They would be discovered for certain now. Try as she might, she couldn't exhale.

The men tossed their loads into the back of the van and slammed the doors closed. They climbed inside the front of the van. It started. Evidently, they had not noticed her mother.

How could that be? Unbelievable!

Fiona didn't know what to do. There was nothing she could do—except follow, she supposed. The van backed out of the parking spot and headed for the intersection. No, they did not run over the cat—it was gone.

Well, at least someone was going to survive this night.

# Thirteen

Now what? Fiona's stomach was in knots. Her stress level was at its limit. Without turning on her headlights, she followed the van, while keeping a distance, allowing it to approach the intersection first. Thankfully, a fresh produce delivery truck pulled up behind it. She turned her headlights on low, and pulled in the turning lane to get on three-seventy-six toward Pittsburgh, behind the truck and the van. Her mind was racing. Where were they going? What would they do when they got to their destination and found her mother in the back of the van?

Double, triple, *quadruple* yikes!

It was official. Her mother's little stakeout operation had blown up in their faces. They were in trouble. They were in the proverbial deep do-do! She had to get her mother out of that van, but how? She needed help, and as much as she dreaded the very thought of calling Nathan to confess what they had done, yet again, she had to.

What did he say about working within the boundaries of the law? She couldn't remember, but she knew this little trick would not qualify—that was for sure.

Hands shaking, she reached for her cell phone sitting in the cup holder. This was it. She had to tell Nathan what was going on. He was going to be so upset. As her fingers tentatively hovered over the cell, it lit up and barked like a little dog, announcing that she'd received a text message from…her mom!

What?

How was she sending a text message from the back of the van?

The bad guys, or drug guys, or dry cleaners would see the illumination from the screen. She'd be found out by the very people who they'd been spying on.

Everyone knows what happens to spies.

Oh, no! Maybe *they* were sending the text, using her mother's phone.

Maybe it was a ransom text from the thugs who were driving.

What would she do then? Her father didn't have millions of dollars to pay a ransom.

Okay, maybe she was overreacting. Maybe it was just a text.

On a steadying breath, she pressed the envelope icon on the screen to read the message:

*I'm under a pile of Santa costumes.*
*From their conversation,*
*I think we're going to Smallman Street.*

It was no mystery that her mother had been a ninth grade English teacher. Even her text message sent during a dire situation was grammatically correct. Yeesh!

Smallman Street…Smallman Street—that's in the strip district, and it was ringing a bell. The light turned green. The van and the truck rolled onto the ramp. Fiona followed.

Smallman Street—now she remembered! Nathan had told her that's where the Santa costumes came from—Characters for All Occasions located on Smallman Street.

Fiona had a solid rule: never text and drive, except this was an emergency. She had no choice—she had to break the rule. It seemed that she'd been breaking a lot of rules lately. Slowing the car to almost a crawl, she texted back: *Who are they?*

Her mother quickly responded: *How should I know? They haven't exactly introduced themselves. They don't know that I'm here, Fiona.*

Fiona rolled her eyes—it was so like her mother to send *that* response. She texted: *Calling Nate.*

Her mom replied: *Not yet! I've got a plan. But I'm so that glad you're considering calling him Nate.*

"Really?" Fiona groaned under her breath—another eye roll was in order.

The only reason she used Nate was because it was shorter for texting. Clearly, her mother had no concept for short texting. She was in the midst of realizing that her mother lacked concept for many things. On top of that, the very last thing she wanted to hear or read was that her mother had yet another plan. She had no idea how they were going to recover from the current plan.

Did she dare ask?

Oh, what the heck? How could things possibly get any worse?

Dumb question. Throwing caution to the wind, she texted: *What plan?*

No response.

The produce truck turned off at the Greentree exit. Fiona was now following the white van down Greentree Hill toward the Fort Pitt Tunnels. She was careful to keep a stealth distance as not to be detected. At this point they were about twelve to fifteen minutes from their destination—maybe less because of the early hour and a reduced amount of traffic.

She waited.

Still nothing from her mother.

Had they discovered her?

Maybe her phone died.

The familiar rumble of tires hitting the enclosed pavement echoed as her Mini Cooper rolled through the tunnel about six car lengths behind the van. When her car emerged on the other side onto the Fort Pitt Bridge, there was still no text from her mom.

Someone once told her that life was all about how one handles plan B. Well, like it or lump it—plan B consisted of calling Nathan. Right. Now.

—m—

"You did *what?*" Nathan Landry blurted into his cell phone, as he bolted up from his pillow. There were no quiet moments of drowsiness or yawning while stretching to awareness. He was instantly awake, rolling out of the bed, grabbing his pants from a nearby chair, and hopping on one foot, while trying to shove the other into the leg after Fiona had just explained her conundrum. "Why would you go to the dry cleaners?"

"I didn't exactly *plan* to go there. I told you, it was completely out of my control. It just sort of happened. I never thought anyone would actually show up at the dry cleaners at three in the morning. And who could've predicted that Keith would jump out of the car, and he and my mother would end up in the back of their van?"

"*Keith Schlemmer's* there?"

"No, the *other* Keith—my mother's dog. Keep up, Nathan!"

Shrugging into his shirt, Nathan sighed. "Why did she get into the van? That's just crazy."

"Because Keith—the dog—ugh! Never mind. I don't have time to defend my mother's sanity, Nathan. What am I supposed to do when they find her back there, if they haven't already?"

He pushed into his shoes, while buttoning his shirt. "We don't have a solid suspect in this case, but it sound like you may have just blown it wide open. Not that I'm happy about this, Fiona. We need to have a serious talk about boundaries." His cell vibrated with another call. The screen announced, Tavia Andrews. "Hold on a minute, Fiona." He pressed the button to switch calls. "What've you got, Tav?"

"It took a little digging through data bases and some of my hacking skills, but I got some serious information," Tavia began. "The shop gets their costumes from Mexico. They are shipped from a woman named Anika Garcia, who owns a costume manufacturing company. Here's the interesting thing about Ms. Garcia, she used to be married to Jose Garcia—sound familiar? He's a huge leader of a drug cartel in Mexico, and during their marriage, Anika learned a lot. Since their divorce, she has become a major player—much to her ex's disgust. We can't touch her, of course, but we can cut off this little connection she's got going in Pittsburgh. Chezmadia's shop ordered all new Santa costumes this year. They're also expecting Easter Bunny costumes and, get this, a shipment of George Washington and Abraham Lincoln costumes in April. Sounds like the pierogi races at the Pirate's games will be a little more exciting this spring."

"The father of our country and Honest Abe?" Nathan said.

"Hey, nothing's sacred anymore."

"I'll bet dollars to donuts the drugs are sewn into the costumes and shipped. Somehow poor Uncle Wilbur got the wrong costume, and they killed him for it," Nathan said.

"You read my mind."

"They must've been looking for more than one misplaced costume. They burgled Mr. Warner's house to get his…unless—"

"Unless what?" Tavia pressed.

"Just a random thought. Sounds like it's time to spread some Christmas joy—stick by the phone. I'll call ya back." Scratching the beard still stuck to his face, and with a plan hatching in his brain, he switched over to his call with Fiona. "Fiona…Tavia just came through with some vital information. Hold on and stay out of sight. I've got a plan in the works."

# Fourteen

The white van was turning onto Smallman Street and still Fiona had not received a text from her mother. What was going on in that van? She wasn't sure she wanted to know the answer. She followed until they drove past the Characters for All Occasions costume shop to turn right into an alley that ran parallel with the shop's building. Fiona gulped back a big braced breath. Were they going into the alley to dispose of her mother? How could she follow them without being noticed? The alley wasn't exactly a busy place—especially at four a.m. They would spot her for sure.

The van rolled down the alleyway. Fiona continued along Smallman, past the alley. She figured there would be another side street down a ways that she could turn into and circle back around. That was as far as her figuring had taken her—she had no idea what she was supposed to do after that. Nathan instructed her to stay out of sight. Okay, but she still wanted to stay as close as possible to her mother.

"What do you mean you still haven't located the last Santa costume? We've got to do the drop today, Bunny," Bobby Schlemmer demanded as he tossed a pile of costumes on the floor of the warehouse area behind the costume shop.

Bunny hurried down a pair of metal stairs from a catwalk above. "I don't know what to tell you, Bobby." She pointed at a piece of paper with a neon pink fingernail. "According to the list Paul gave me, we got Wilbur's costume. Not the way we wanted to, but we did get it, and yes, the drugs were there. Where's the list I gave Nonatha to give to you? She gave it to you, didn't she?"

"Yeah, she did—and that's another thing you shouldn't have done. Don't give vital information—especially handwritten information, to someone who isn't involved. Why do we have handwritten lists anyway? Why aren't we texting this information?"

Bunny lifted a shoulder. "Paul's old school. He doesn't like texting. I don't think he knows how."

"He'd better learn if we're gonna continue working with this lady. She's bigtime—real bigtime."

"Whatever, Bobby. I think it's okay. There's no way Nonatha knew what the list was—no one would. Anyway, where is it?"

He shrugged. "I threw it out, I think."

"And you're yellin' at me? Anyone could'a found that list."

"Thought you just said no one would know what the list was for," Bobby said, curtly.

She blew out a frustrated breath. "Come here. I'll show you. See? SN-100 is crossed off *my* list—the list I still have. We collected Pete's costume, SN-1000, he's Ross Park—got the drugs. Tom, the Santa at South Hills Village, SN-301—yep. Brian at Monroeville, check. Ed at the Waterworks—got it. I thought we got the Beaver Valley costume. I crossed it off, but we're still one costume short—or maybe they shorted us some of the drugs in the shipment."

"No way. They've done just like they said they would. Four boxes of costumes. Eight costumes per box. Six laced with the stuff. This is your fault, Bunny. I should'a never let you handle the shipment. I should'a just had you remove the drugs like we originally agreed," Bobby bit out.

"Look, I'm sorry. I got confused. It was easy to do. Some of those numbers on the packing labels look the same. How was I to know I sent five costumes carrying the stuff out to the Santas? I just feel so bad that one of them got killed cuz of it."

"Hey! That old boy had no business waving a gun around. I didn't mean to hurt him. I was just trying to take it off of him. If he'd just let Paul borrow the costume, none of this would've happened—none of the other Santas would let him borrow their costumes either. Whatta pain!"

Bunny shrugged. "Can't blame them. Jim's rule about replacing the costume if you lose it prob'ly had them all worried. I mean, who wants to replace something you don't own to begin with?"

"Doesn't matter now. Breaking into his house was a bad idea to begin with. We should 'a just did what we started doing after that—taking them from the old guys at the malls for cleaning. No one would've figured it out, and no one would've got hurt."

"You mean killed. Too late now, Bobby," Bunny said. "At least they don't suspect, cuz we robbed Paul's house too. If ol' Wilbur wouldn't have got killed, we could'a just robbed the other Santas—bet we would've come up with the costumes real quick."

"That's just not what went down, and yeah, I bet they suspect," Bobby said. "I wonder where Paul is—I just sent him out to the van to get some of the costumes. What's taking him so long?"

Bunny giggled. "He's prob'ly having' a smoke."

"Hey!" a voice called from the door. "We've got a big problem, Bobby."

Bunny and Bobby turned to see Paul Warner dragging a red-headed woman, carrying a small dog, into the warehouse.

Bunny's eyes widened. "I know you. You were one of the cat burglars in jail with me the other night."

Nancy smiled. "That's right! You were dressed like an elf."

Bunny giggled. "Yep! That was me."

"I found her under the costumes in the back of the van," Paul said. "I don't know how or when she got in there. Don't you people lock your van at night? What are we gonna do with her?"

Planting his hands on his hips, Bobby's brows furrowed. He drew closer to the woman. "Nancy? Nancy Burrell?"

Nancy yanked her arm from Paul's grasp. "I can't believe it, Bobby. You should be ashamed of yourself. I thought the Schlemmer boys were nice guys. Wow, was I wrong. Guess I made the right choice when I married Garrett. I would never have wanted to be a mobster's wife."

"What is she talkin' about? Who is she? Who's Garrett? What's goin' on, Bobby?" Paul demanded to know as a fit of relentless coughs broke out.

"She's my brother's old girlfriend," Bobby said.

Nancy let out an affronted gasp. "Who are you calling *old*? And I was not just his girlfriend. I was his *fiancé*—until I dumped him for Garrett Quinn. Best decision I ever made. Now the Schlemmers are out murdering sweet old men, like my poor Uncle Wilbur. What could he possibly have done to deserve such a thing?"

Bobby flinched back. "Wilbur Stacy was your uncle? Look, Nancy, it was an accident. I didn't mean to kill him. I swear."

"This is not good, Bobby. Not good at all," Paul said, as he gasp for air, while hacking and choking.

"Aw, go get your oxygen tank, Paul. We've got more problems than just an ol—er, a girlfriend from my brother's past showin' up. We're still missin' some inventory, and we gotta find it quick. Our connection will be expecting us real soon, and we'd better have all the stuff."

Bunny ran her fingers over Keith's ears. "What's your doggie's name?"

"Keith," Nancy replied only to have Bobby's gaze flick to meet hers. "As in Keith Richards—of the Rolling Stones. Big fan—I was a *big* fan. It has nothing to do with your brother, believe me."

Indeed Fiona found another alley to cut through to circle back toward the costume shop. She dropped her headlights down to parking lights as she slowly rolled the Mini Cooper along the rear side of businesses along the strip. She found it most peculiar how she noticed something she never really paid much attention to in the past—dumpsters, and there were lots of them.

It wasn't long until she came close to the docking area for Characters for All Occasions. She parked along the alley. She could see the white van sitting outside a door beside the dock. The doors to the van were open as was the door that led into what looked like a warehouse space attached to the back of the shop. The lights were on inside the warehouse, but she couldn't see what was going on beyond the door.

Feeling confident that she was far enough away as to not be noticed, Fiona clung to her cell phone hoping to hear from Nathan or her mother. She turned her parking lights off, and laid her head against the headrest, closing her eyes. Trying to calm down, she hoped her mother was okay, and everything would be fine in the end. Try as she might, she couldn't stop her mind from racing. She opened her eyes to keep watch over the dock.

Wait a minute.

Could it be that they were thinking about this all wrong?

They'd focused the investigation on the dry cleaner because she'd found the note in their dumpster, but maybe the dry cleaner was simply transporting the costumes from one place to another for the costume company. Uncle Wilbur told her his costume was brand new. The Santa's she and Nathan spoke to seemed genuinely baffled as to why the costumes had to be turned in for cleaning—as was her uncle. The cocaine had to be inside the costumes somehow, and somehow the costumes got into the wrong hands—Santa Claus's hands.

Her eyes widened. Her body stiffened in the seat.

That's it!

The drug runners were looking for a costume that had been handed out to one or more of the Santa's by mistake. That's why they burgled the Santa from Crafton, and they were trying to loot Uncle Wilbur's home, and took nothing but the costumes—they were searching for a particular costume. Only Uncle Wilbur walked in on his burglar, and unfortunately, Wilbur tried to defend his castle—unsuccessfully.

Now the essential questions remained: Who was putting the cocaine in the costumes? When was the cocaine inserted? More importantly, where were the costumes actually coming from? Where were they manufactured?

Fiona tended to be on the conservative side when it came to using her data plan. Now was not the time to for conservation—now was the time for information. She pulled up search engines on her phone looking for companies who manufacture costumes. It was more likely that the drugs would be coming from out of the country—at least it always seems like they do, so she searched the internet for costume manufacturers outside of the US.

Instantly, an article that had just been posted that very morning along with a man's photograph popped up: Jose Garcia. He had been arrested in Mexico overnight. He was a drug lord the Mexican authorities had been watching for quite some time. They apprehended him and most of his cartel, claiming the bust to be one of the biggest in many years. The photograph that had been posted was several years old. Okay, why did this particular post and photo come up on her search? She read a little farther—his wife, Anika Garcia, who was in the photo, was a character costume designer. She produced most of the mascot style costumes for many of the teams in the good ol' US of A!

Was Anika Garcia the connection they'd been looking for? Fiona began to dial Nathan.

There was a tap on the window. Fiona flinched. An older man with a mobile oxygen tank at his side gestured for her to put her window down. She hesitated. He smiled and said something that she couldn't decipher through the glass.

He appeared harmless enough so Fiona pressed the button to lower the window. "Excuse me?"

"This is a no parking zone, ma'am," the man said, and then he shoved his arm through the window to grab the door latch and yank the door open. Fiona gasped. He grabbed her by the arm to drag her from the vehicle. "Who are you, and what are you doing here?"

Fiona tried to pull away. "I...I'm just sitting here waiting for someone!"

"Yeah, and I'm your aunt Martha. I saw this Cooper followin' our van since Greentree Hill," the man said, while trying to suppress a cough. Suddenly, he was pointing something at her through the pocket of his jacket. Tersely, he asked, "Are you with the cops?"

"I don't know what you're talking about! I was just coming this way!" She tried to tug her arm from his grip, but even through the fit of coughing, he managed to dig his fingers into her arm all the more.

"Whatever, sister. You're comin' with me!" Coughing and hacking, the man shoved her roughly toward the costume shop. Ditching the oxygen tank, he directed her with what she worried was a gun in his pocket up the short set of steps and into the warehouse. Pushing her through the door, he called out, "We've got double trouble, Bobby. Who's this? Your brother's love child?"

Bobby, Bunny, and Fiona's mother turned to see Fiona in the crusty old guy's custody.

"Hey! That's the other cat burglar!" Bunny announced.

"We are *not* cat burglars! Mom, did you tell them that we're cat burglars?" Fiona demanded.

"No, she figured it out for herself. I told you, this is exactly what cat burglars wear. Honestly, no one in my family ever gives me credit for knowing anything." Her mother gesturing to the dark clothing that she and Fiona were sporting.

"I agree," Bunny said. "That's what every cat burglar that I've ever known wore."

"Oh, my God, you're fanning the flame! Never mind that. Why did you jump into the back of the van? Are you out of your mind?" Fiona more demanded than asked.

"Where else was I supposed to go?"

"Anywhere! Anywhere but in the back of the van! Now we're in big trouble—on so many levels. And why did you stop texting me? Do you have any idea how worried I was that they had killed you?"

Her mother shrugged. "My phone went dead. What was I supposed to do? Send up a smoke signal?"

Bobby stepped between the two women. "Wait a minute! You're *her* daughter?"

"I'm afraid so," Fiona said, crossing her arms over her chest, while turning away from her mother.

His face filled with trepidation, Bobby spun around toward Fiona's mother to inquire, "She isn't…I mean, please tell me that she isn't my brother's—"

"What kind of a girl do you think I was, Bobby?" her mom asked. Feigning insult, she turned away, crossing her arms over her chest, too.

Frustrated, confused, and overwhelmed, Bobby scrubbed his forehead with nervous fingers. "Look…we gotta figure out what we're gonna do about this—"

"No, Bobby! *You* gotta figure it out. This sounds like family problems. Bunny and me are goin' out front to count the costumes again—see if we missed one. You take care of this mess, and you'd better take care of it right quick," Paul told him, as he and Bunny stepped through the door that led into the store.

"Now what?" Fiona asked in a shaky voice.

"I suppose he's going to kill us," her mother said. "He killed Uncle Wilbur. Why wouldn't he kill us too?"

"He killed Uncle Wilbur?"

"Now wait a minute, Nancy! I told you that was an accident! I didn't mean for that to happen," Bobby said.

"Well it did happen! You seem confused as to what you should do. I think you should do the *right* thing—turn yourself in," Fiona's mom said.

"Is that what you think?"

"Oh! I know! Why don't you call Keith, and see what he thinks you should do? He was always getting you out of trouble. Remember that time you backed into your father's brand new Cadillac? It was Keith who got the plunger and pulled out the big dent. Oh! And remember when you—"

"I can't call Keith! He doesn't know a thing about all this. He's not involved in any way. Other than he cleaned the costumes so there wouldn't be any trace of the cocaine, but he didn't know he was doing that. He just thought he was cleaning Jimmy's costumes. Look, I don't want to hurt you, Nancy, or your little daughter here, but I can't have you two reporting all this to the police."

"Too late, Bobby. Fiona's boyfriend is a homicide detective, and he's hot on your trail!" Fiona's mother blurted out, angrily.

Bobby's mouth dropped open. He pulled a gun from the back of his waistband to train it on the two women. Hugging her dog closer to her chest, Fiona's mother gasped.

"That was helpful, Mom. That was *really* helpful," Fiona groaned.

"Ho! Ho! Ho! Merry Christmas!" A voice boomed through the warehouse, bouncing off the block walls.

Muddled and panicked by the sudden echo, Bobby whipped around to find Santa Claus standing in the dock's doorway, flanked by two elves.

Fiona and her mother's eyes brightened at the sight of Nathan clad in the cheap Santa costume he'd worn to entertain the kindergarten class the day before. To his right, Tavia made an adorable elf, while to his left, Wyatt made for an overtly tall elf who appeared very uncomfortable in a pair of green tights.

Tail wagging, ears perked, Keith let out an ornery bark.

"What have we here?" Nathan/Santa asked. "Looks like someone's been very naughty!"

Trying to keep his eye on the two women, while trying to comprehend the strangers in the doorway, Bobby swung his handgun from group to group. "What the—get outta here! The bars are down the street a block. You're in the wrong place, ya stupid drunks! Now get outta here before I shoot you!"

"Lord knows he's got plenty of experience," Fiona's mom mumbled.

"*Mom—*"

"You wouldn't shoot Santa, would you, Bobby?" Nathan/Santa asked. "Anika wouldn't like that too much. She sent us for the stuff. Her clients want it early. They've decided to get out of Pittsburgh for the holiday, so she sent Santa and his elves to do the drop for you. You got the stuff, right? Cuz we wouldn't want a problem on Christmas Eve, would we?"

After taking a step back, Bobby stilled. "Anika sent you?"

Nathan/Santa looked all around. "Is there an echo in here?"

"Yeah, there is," Wyatt grumbled.

"I thought I said something about Anika Garcia sending us for the stuff." He glanced at Wyatt, who was scowling, while tugging at his tights. "My very tall elf is getting grouchy. Looks like we got him the wrong pair of tights. That's what we get for shopping at Walmart. You got the stuff or not, Schlemmer?"

Bobby aimed the gun at Nathan/Santa. "How do I know you're really with Anika? How do I know yinz' aren't the cops?"

Nathan/Santa turned to Tavia. "Son estás ropa demasiado apretada?"

Cocking her head to one side, Tavia narrowed her eyes, while furrowing her brows. She mouthed, "What?"

Fiona's mother whispered in her ear, "What did he just ask her?"

"My Spanish is a little rusty, but I'm pretty sure he asked her if her underwear was too tight," Fiona whispered back.

"Why would he ask her that?"

"It's Nathan. Who knows what he's doing." Fiona said around a sigh.

Realizing that his question was not only wrong, but by Tavia's reaction, inappropriate as well, Nathan/Santa back-peddled. "She's new. Let me try again." He cleared his throat, and using exaggerated gestures, he said, "Call-o on your cello-phono, Anika Garcia."

Pitching him a baleful look, Tavia muttered, "Si, si, Senor-O." She made a big show of digging for her cell phone through the elf skirt into her tights. Upon retrieving the phone, she punched a few buttons. She held the phone to her ear, while tapping her elf shoe as if she were impatiently waiting for Anika to pick up. The bells on the toes jingled with every strike to the floor. Her face brightened. She asked, "Estás listo?" She smiled and nodded. "Gracias." She handed the phone to Nathan/Santa.

Placing the phone against his chest as if he didn't want Anika to hear his conversation, he asked, "You did say that you have the stuff, right? I mean, I don't want to tell her that everything's a go only to find out you're not properly prepared. That would make her very angry. You do know what happens when Anika gets angry, don't you?"

Bobby's brow was now saturated in sweat. It was dripping down his temples and into his eyes. He wiped it away with a shaking hand. "Look...there's been a little glitch. We're missing one of the costumes that had the stuff in it. We're looking for it now, and I'm sure we'll find it any minute. We just need a little more time. Not much, mind you, just a little."

"Like...how much time?"

Bobby glanced all around the warehouse. His eyes snapped toward the door that led into the main store. It was obvious what he was thinking—where were his partners?

Finally, he managed, "I...I don't know. I sent my friends to take another look in the store, but they haven't come back. I...I don't know what's taking so long."

"Uh, oh, maybe they couldn't find the stuff and bailed out on you," Nathan/Santa suggested.

"No! No, they wouldn't do that. They're in for the long haul. I'm tellin' ya, we've got the stuff—at least most of it. Just give us a little more time. An...an hour or so, that's all I'm askin' for. I'm sure it'll turn up. I'm sure of it!"

Stroking his beard woefully, Nathan/Santa shook his head. "I'd really like to help ya, buddy, really I would, but Anika has strict rules about this stuff." He spoke more loudly, "You're *sure* you don't know where the stuff is?"

"Is this what you're looking for, Bobby?" A voice bellowed from above.

Bobby swiveled on his heels to look up toward the catwalk where he found Jim Chezmadia surrounded in a cloud of thick smoke. Through the miasma it was clear that he was holding up a Santa

Costume on a hanger. The white fur that once lined the bottom of the coat was torn away, dangling by threads.

Pulling a cigar from his lips, Jim growled, "Your friend, Bernadette, who I was stupid enough to hire, left this on the railing outside my office yesterday. Imagine my surprise when I noticed a white powdery substance leaking from the fur. Now, imagine my anger when I yanked the fur off to find bags of cocaine sewn all through one of my brand new Santa costumes."

"Listen, Jimmy! These guys need that stuff! They're gonna kill me and Paul and Bunny if you don't hand it over!" Bobby begged.

Angrily, Jim pitched the costume over the railing of the catwalk. It floated to the cement floor below. "Don't you get it, Bobby? I was woke up by police pounding on my door at three-thirty this morning. They wanted to arrest me. When I told them what happened, and that I was planning on confronting you myself because I was crazy enough to think that maybe you'd do the right thing and turn yourself in. They then informed me they were gonna have a drug raid at my shop! They're not gonna kill you! They're police officers, you idiot!" He jerked his thumb over his shoulder. "There's a whole bunch of them in the store right now, ripping it apart, looking for more costumes laced with drugs! They've got Paul and Bernadette in custody! I'm gonna lose my entire inventory because of you! I can't believe you'd do this, Bobby! I just can't believe it!" Using the cigar, Jim pointed at the Santa standing near his stepbrother on the Warehouse floor. "Book 'em, Danno!"

"Landry... I'm Detective Nathan Landry."

"Whatever!"

Immediately, the huge garage door lifted, the door that led into the store burst open, a SWAT team with guns trained on Bobby stepped into the warehouse. Several SWAT members joined Jim on the catwalk.

"It's over. Drop the gun, Bobby," Nathan/Santa said.

Bobby complied immediately. As the gun hit the cement, his hands raised in surrender.

As Nathan/Santa clamped handcuffs to his wrists, he said, "Robert Schlemmer, you're under arrest for possession and distribution of an illegal drug—"

"And the murder of Wilbur Stacy!" Fiona declared. Nathan/Santa's gaze snapped to meet hers. "He confessed to my mother and I just moments ago."

"I see. In that case, you're also under arrest for the murder of Santa Claus."

## Fifteen

The front door opened quickly. Too quickly for Nathan. He fell through the opening and almost on top of Nancy as she was exiting the house, while he was attempting to enter.

"Oh! Nate! Are you okay?" Nancy said, grabbing his arm in an effort to steady him.

"Sorry! I didn't realize you were opening the door." He noticed the bottle of wine in her hand and the lovely emerald green long sleeved sheath dress she was wearing. "Don't you look beautiful? Going somewhere special for Christmas Eve?"

"Fiona's letting us borrow her car," she giggled. "Isn't that a switch? Some of our old friends in the neighborhood are getting together for a Christmas Eve wine tasting. I'm so excited. I haven't seen some of these people in over two years. We'll be going home to Florida right after the new year, so we want to make sure we visit a bit." She held up a photo. "I can't wait to show off this adorable picture of you and Fiona on Santa's lap."

Nathan smiled.

Garrett stepped into the foyer from the living room with a pack of Yorkies at his heels. Nathan shook his hand. "Well, you two have a great time. I think Fiona and I are planning a quiet evening in." He peeked into the living room. The tree glimmered, yet the star still stood at the apex—unlit. "Still not allowing anyone to replace that dark star, I see."

"Not yet," Garrett said. "Maybe next year."

Winking, Nancy told him, "Well, you two have a lovely evening, and don't do anything that I wouldn't do."

"Whoa, that leaves the evening wide open," Nathan pointed out around a chuckle.

Nancy shot him a knowing grin, tossed her evening wrap around her shoulders, and stepped out into the chilly night. Making sure that no dogs escaped, Garrett followed.

Fiona came down the stairs carrying Harriet in her arms. The little Maltese's hair was gathered on top of her head and tied with a bright red Christmas bow.

He tickled the dog's cheek. "Don't you look cute for Christmas, Harriet?" Fiona set the dog down among the Yorkies. He added, "Wait a minute. Some of the Yorkies are wearing bows too. What's going on?"

Pointing at the nearest Yorkie, Fiona said, "That's George."

Nathan shot her a raised eyebrow.

She giggled. "George happens to be a girl. I just realized it today—hence the bow." Hitching her chin toward another Yorkie, she said, "By the way, Ringo's a girl too."

Nathan laughed. "Why am I not surprised? Keith's a boy, right?"

"Yes, he is," Fiona snorted. "But, get this, Mom's thinking about changing his name."

Surprised, Nathan blinked back. "Seriously? I'm almost afraid to ask, to what?"

"Sting."

He scooped up the Yorkie, formally known as Keith, and looked into his face. "Ya know, it works. Hey, Keith, looks like you're gonna be a rock star after all."

"It looks that way." She smiled. "Too bad you had to miss the service this afternoon. It was very nice. Uncle Wilbur would have been pleased. We sang some of his favorite Christmas songs, including, Here Comes Santa Claus. I think he would've liked that most of all."

"I think so too. I'm sorry I missed it. I was a little tied up with all the paperwork involved with all the arrests we made today in Wilbur's case. It was a very productive day. I'm glad we were able to solve his murder, close down a small drug ring, and we even apprehended the thugs who were going to be on the receiving end of the cocaine. That Bunny just can't keep a secret. She sang like a canary. Paul Warner and Bob Schlemmer had no idea who they'd gotten involved with." Nathan said, setting Sting—the Yorkie formerly known as Keith to the floor.

"Is that why everyone on the police force knows Bunny?"

He snorted. "Yep. Too bad. Whether she knew it or not, Bunny was a great informant. Now she'll be going away for quite some time on drug charges and accessory to murder charges—which is really a shame. Bunny wouldn't hurt anyone, and even though she wasn't actually present, she was part of your uncle's murder. The really sad part was Bunny was truly remorseful about your uncle's death. Unfortunately, we don't see a lot of that."

"Mm. So what about Anika Garcia?"

"What about her? We can't touch her, but as you know, her ex-husband was arrested in Mexico. Will they be able to keep hold of him? Who knows? But I have a feeling they are well aware of Anika's activities. They'll be informed of what went on here in Pittsburgh. It'll only a matter of time until they nab her, I hope."

"I hope it's sooner than later."

Fiona took a big whiff of the air. The rich aroma of fresh coffee perking wafted into the foyer. Tilting her head to one side, she stilled, and then asked, "Did you make coffee?"

"No. I just got here."

Fiona rushed into the kitchen. From its station on the counter, the coffeemaker was gurgling and popping. Dark coffee was streaming into the carafe. Her eyes brightened with delight at the sight. "Um...did mom make coffee?"

"I don't know. I doubt it. They were walking out the door when I came in." Fiona stared at the coffeemaker with wide-eyed wonder. "It's just coffee, Fiona. Would you like some? I'll pour it for you."

"Yeah...yeah, I'll get the cups." She pulled two mugs from the cabinets.

He poured the coffee, while she gathered the creamer and sugar. Once the coffees were prepped, they walked hand in hand into the living room and sat on the couch. The lights from the tree filled the room with a cozy Christmas glow. Fiona stared at her mug thoughtfully.

"Are you gonna drink it or are you getting ready to interrogate it?" Nathan asked.

Fiona snuggled deeper in the couch, lifting her mug to her lips. "I'm drinking it." She took a sip, and then with a demure smile on her lips, she asked, "Nathan…when are you going to remove that beard?"

He scratched at it. "I'll start working on it when I go home tonight. It's really starting to itch. My natural whiskers are growing underneath."

"I imagine so." She cleared her throat. "Nathan…why haven't you introduced me to your mother?"

His fingers stilled inside the faux beard. He pondered the question for a moment. "I dunno. It just never happened. Do you want to meet her?"

"Yes…no…I don't know."

"Well, that certainly make things all neat and tidy. I'll gladly introduce you, if you want. She doesn't bite or anything like that."

"I want to meet her. It's just that I'm not sure I'm quite ready. Although, it seems unfair. I mean, you've met my crazy family. You've even had to solve a murder for them." She thought about it for a moment. "Yes, I should meet your mom," Fiona said, her tone and body language coinciding with the commitment to her decision.

"Consider it done."

"Um…Nathan…one more thing…I was wondering, would you rather I call you Nate?"

He snorted. "Why would you do that?"

"My mom calls you Nate. Do you want me to?"

"Some of my friends call me Nate. It's the casual version of my name, I suppose. That said, I don't think there's anything casual about our relationship, Fiona. Do you?"

Fiona couldn't have hid the smile on her mouth if she wanted to. Her heart swelled. "No, *Nathan*, I don't think there's anything casual about the way I feel for you."

He pulled her close and kissed her lips. Suddenly the room was filled with glorious illumination. Fiona pulled back from the kiss. Her eyes widened. Her mouth dropped open. The star on the top of the tree was shining brighter than it ever had before.

"Well, would you look at that?" Nathan said. "I told you Christmas would turn out just fine."

Tears filled her eyes as she pulled him into a tight hug. "You sure did. Merry Christmas, Nathan." Over his shoulder she lifted her coffee mug into a toast, and mouthed toward the tree, "Merry Christmas, Grandma, and welcome back."

Through the window Fiona could see a soft snow beginning to fall—Christmas would be almost perfect after all.

### *END*

Thank you for reading *Merry Murder*. Join Fiona and the gang for a hot whodunit on the sandy beaches of Presque Isle, Pennsylvania! Coming spring of 2017—*On Waves of Murder!* For more information on C.S. McDonald and her books, please visit her website: www.csmcdonaldbooks.com

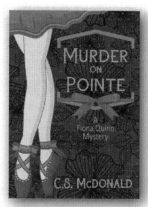

**MURDER ON POINTE**

Book #1 from Fiona Quinn

Fiona Quinn can't wait to attend the performance of Coppelia at the Benedum Center in Pittsburgh. Her old friend, Silja Ramsay, is dancing the lead role. They have dinner after the show. When they return, Pittsburgh Ballet Theater is down one ballerina. Principal dancer, Alexis Cartwright, has been murdered in her dressing room!

Is this murder a result of hot tempers among members of the cast? Or is this a random act of violence? Will there be more? Police detective, Nathan Landry, isn't taking any chances. After finding out that Fiona has a strong ballet background, he recruits her to go undercover among the cast of Coppelia.

Can Fiona help catch the killer or will she be the next victim?

*Everyone loves Fiona!*

"McDonald keeps readers guessing and second-guessing... A totally, enjoyable quick read that pulls you in from first to last page!" ~G. Bixler Reviews

"Right on point!" ~Fran Lewis Reviews

"Delightful from beginning to end!" ~Sherry Wilson/Amazon customer

Hey! Don't forget the

Children's books by C.S. McDonald

Delightful stories with wonderful lessons—your kids
will love George!

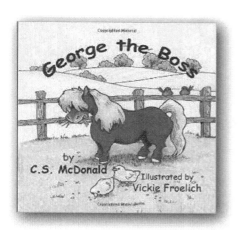

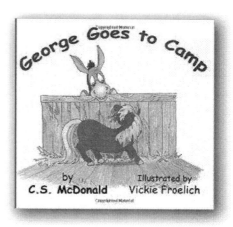

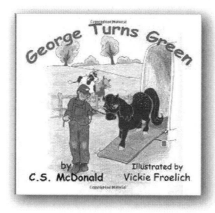

## About C.S. McDonald

For twenty-six years C.S. McDonald's life whirled around a song and a dance. She was a professional dancer and choreographer. During that time she choreographed many musicals and an opera for the Pittsburgh Savoyards. In 2011 she retired from her dance career to write. Under her real name, Cindy McDonald, she writes murder-suspense and romantic suspense novels. In 2014 she added the pen name, C.S. McDonald, to write children's books for her grandchildren. Now she adds the Fiona Quinn Mysteries to that expansion. She decided to write the cozy mystery series for her young granddaughters.

Ms. McDonald resides on her Thoroughbred farm known as Fly by Night Stables near Pittsburgh, Pennsylvania with her husband, Bill, and her poorly behaved Cocker Spaniel, Allister.

You can learn more about C.S. McDonald and her books here: www.csmcdonaldbooks.com

Made in the USA
San Bernardino, CA
16 September 2016